BAD BLOOD

Deputy US Marshal Cal Burnett rides into Pike's Peak, Kansas, after an absence of ten years, expecting to find the town as he had left it. Any hopes of this are quickly destroyed, though. Strange and disturbing rumours reach him: his brother, Lance, has disappeared, and people say he robbed the local bank before skipping town. Cal begins to investigate, but it's when he meets the local law — Sheriff Snark and his deputy Rufus Hoyle — that his troubles really begin . . .

CORBA SUNMAN

BAD BLOOD

Complete and Unabridged

LINFORD
Leicester

First published in Great Britain in 2015 by
Robert Hale Limited
London

First Linford Edition
published 2018
by arrangement with
Robert Hale
an imprint of The Crowood Press
Wiltshire

A catalogue record for this book is available
from the British Library.

ISBN 978–1–4448–3665–3

Published by
F. A. Thorpe (Publishing)
Anstey, Leicestershire

Set by Words & Graphics Ltd.
Anstey, Leicestershire
Printed and bound in Great Britain by
T. J. International Ltd., Padstow, Cornwall

This book is printed on acid-free paper

1

Cal Burnett rode into Pike's Crossing, Kansas just before noon and traversed the busy street to the livery barn. He reined his bay aside as a stage coach approached from the opposite direction, raising dust and scattering townsfolk to the sidewalks. The coach pulled up outside the Wells Fargo office next to the bank and the driver jumped off his high seat, hollering that he had been held up and robbed and that the shotgun guard was lying dead inside the vehicle. Burnett passed the coach as a crowd gathered and continued on his way. He felt out of place as townsfolk passed him although, as a youth, he had lived on his grandfather's B7 cattle ranch just out of town.

He was aged twenty-eight, stood two inches over six feet; he was big, sturdy, well-muscled, and wore a light blue suit. A tied-down six-gun was on his right thigh, nestling in a greased holster on a cartridge belt that glinted with bright shells in its loops. Folks always took him for a gunslinger, but he had not shot anyone outside the call of duty since the Civil War, now ten years past. He was a deputy US marshal.

But appearances counted, and he was aware that most men gave him plenty of space. His blue eyes were hard and cold, like shards of broken glass, and the harsh expression on his tanned face gave tacit warning to his fellow men that it would be wise to avoid uninvited contact. A black string tie completed his appearance. His dusty Stetson was grey.

He stepped down from his saddle outside the livery barn and paused at the water trough just outside the main entrance to permit his horse to drink. His pale eyes missed nothing of his surroundings. The life he had led since the war, in which he had served as a blue-coat lieutenant in the cavalry, had taken him all over the States as a lawman, but now, still recovering from wounds received in his last assignment, he had decided finally to visit the B7 ranch that he had inherited from his grandfather. Ten years had passed since he last saw the place; his younger brother, Lance, had taken over the running of the business.

An old man appeared in the doorway of the barn, and Burnett recognized him immediately despite the differences in appearance the passing years had laid upon him.

'Bill Fray,' he said. 'How are you doing these days?'

Fray looked up quickly, his expression turning bleak as he studied the imposing figure confronting him. He shook his head slowly.

'You've got the better of me, mister,' he said at length. 'You talk like you know me, but I doubt I ever set eyes on you before. By the look of you I'd say you're riding for Big G. They've been hiring fast guns and building up for trouble.'

'I guess I've changed a lot in the last ten years,' Burnett said. 'But you're sure to recall my name — Cal Burnett. My grandpa, Sam Burnett, owned the B7 ranch.'

Fray's expression changed and his jaw dropped as recognition filled his brown eyes. He nodded slowly, his pent-up breath escaping in a long sigh.

'Yeah, I can see your likeness to old Sam. Well, you're a sight for sore eyes! What brings you back this way after so long? I thought you were killed in the war. Your brother said as much while he was running B7, but you know Lance. He was always close-mouthed. Do you know he was run off the spread earlier this year? He ain't been seen around since.'

'That's news to me.' Burnett's expression did not change. 'Who ran him out?'

'There's only one outfit causes trouble around here. But if you want

4

details you'd better drop in at the law office and have a word with Sheriff Snark. It ain't for the likes of me to run off at the lip. A man could get hisself killed for just looking sideways at a Big G rider. You better watch your step around here, Cal.'

'Thanks for the tip. I reckon I'd better change my plans. See you later, old-timer.'

'Say, you ain't gonna ride out to B7, are you?' Fray demanded in alarm.

'Why shouldn't I? It is my ranch.'

'If that's on your mind then forget it. You'll be committing suicide.'

'I'll play my cards according to the game.' Burnett spoke grimly as he gathered up his reins. He swung into the saddle and headed out of town, riding the trail which he well remembered from his past.

Burnett considered as he rode, wondering what kind of trouble had caused his brother to pull out. There was bad blood between Lance and the rest of the Burnett family because he had gone over to the Confederates when the war started, but Cal had kept an open mind despite fighting the Rebels for three years. When they got back after the war, Lance found that he had been branded a renegade and was treated like poison, but Cal had given his brother the chance to run B7 because his duties as a lawman kept him from living at home.

He kept his law badge in a small pouch sewn inside the left-hand pocket of his jacket, for his law work usually entailed working under cover. He looked around, alert, as he rode the familiar trail, his thoughts brooding over the trouble that Lance had found. His brother was the type who always seemed to fall into trouble, but he would never run away from a fight. And he had disappeared six months ago. Burnett frowned and shook his head. He would not be surprised if he discovered that Lance was dead . . .

As Burnett remembered it, the B7 ranch was a fair-sized spread that supported around two thousand head of cattle. Five miles out of town he reached a left fork in the trail and followed it, aware that he was now on B7 range. He headed for the ranch buildings, hidden from view by a ridge, and pushed his horse into a faster pace because he was suddenly struck by impatience — he had been away a long time.

He topped the ridge and reined in for his first sight of the home buildings; a bitter sigh escaped him when he saw smoke-blackened ruins where the house and barns had stood. He looked around in disbelief, shocked by the grim sight, and for a moment he wondered if he had followed the wrong trail. This could not be B7. He kneed his horse into motion and rode down the reverse slope of the ridge, his mind protesting against the reality of his gaze and anger beginning to smoulder.

The gate to the yard still had a board above it bearing the sign B7 — SAM BURNETT. He reined in and studied it for several moments, and then rode across the yard to stop before the ruins that had once been his home. He stepped down from his saddle and trailed his reins.

Unaccustomed emotion welled up in his breast and he suppressed a sigh. He walked into the ruins and looked around, seeing in his mind how it had looked in the past. He walked through to the kitchen and then out to the rear. Nothing had been spared; the two barns had been burned, and even the posts of the corral had been uprooted.

The silence was complete. He could hear a meadow lark trilling high above his head, and then he caught the sound of approaching hoofs and jerked himself from his nostalgia. He went through to the front yard, his hand on the butt of his gun. Two riders were coming into the yard; one of them held a rifle across his thighs, ready for action. Burnett drew his pistol to be on even terms, held it down by his side, and moved across to his horse in case there was trouble.

The riders were big men, hard-faced, sharp-eyed; well-armed. They halted feet away from Burnett, and he was keenly aware that the man holding the rifle was covering him with the weapon. They were dressed in range clothes. He recalled Bill Fray telling him that the Big G ranch was suspected of causing all the trouble in the county.

'I'll be obliged if you'll point your rifle in another direction,' Burnett said in a rasping tone.

'Who in hell are you?' the man countered truculently. He was dark-eyed; face harshly set. He did not move his rifle. 'This is Big G range. You're on private property. What do you want?'

'I'm inspecting what's left of my property, so you can tell me what you're doing, trespassing,' Burnett replied. He eased his right elbow forward until it was resting lightly on his right hip, and the muzzle of his .45 pistol pointed at the ground just in front of the riders. 'I'm Cal Burnett, and this, to my knowledge, is the B7 ranch.'

'It belongs to Big G now, and we are Big G riders. It's our job to run trespassers out, and that is what you are, so you're in big trouble, mister.'

'I asked you to point your rifle elsewhere,' Burnett grated. 'You better do it right now.'

The man grinned and pushed the muzzle of his rifle a couple of inches towards Burnett, but did not shift his aim. His trigger finger tightened, and Burnett saw the knuckle turning white. The other man did not move a muscle, but his harsh voice sounded in a flat undertone.

'Shoot him in the belly, Hank.'

Burnett flipped up his pistol and fired. The crash of the shot thundered. The bullet smacked into Hank's right shoulder and he reeled in the saddle, dropping his rifle before falling sideways. He hit the ground and lay motionless. Burnett covered the other rider, who sat motionless in a paralysis of shock, his mouth gaping.

'Get rid of your gun,' Burnett snapped, 'and be careful how you do it.'

The man lifted his Colt from its holster and dropped it on the ground. He raised his hands shoulder high without being told. Burnett went forward and kicked away the rifle dropped by the man he had shot.

'So you ride for Big G,' he commented. 'What's your name?'

'I'm Rafe Callow.'

'Who is he? And why did you advise him to shoot me? I told you I own this place, so I have a legal right to be here.'

'He's Hank Millett, and he was on the point of shooting you, anyway.' Callow's broad shoulders lifted in a shrug. 'Have you killed him?'

'Get down and check him out. If he's dead, throw him over his saddle. We'll ride into Pike's Crossing and you can explain to the sheriff what happened here. Who owns Big G?'

'Amos Grint is the boss. He won't be happy when he hears about this.' Callow dismounted and bent over Millett. He looked up at Burnet, smiling grimly. 'He's alive. You'll be sorry you came here today.'

'Keep your mouth shut. All I want to hear from you are answers to my questions.'

'Were you in on the rustling raid that hit Big G last night?' Callow demanded.

'I don't know anything about rustling. All I'm interested in is B7. What happened to my brother Lance when Grint took over this place?'

'As far as I know Grint bought the place legally. There was a bit of trouble when Lance Burnett wouldn't leave peaceably.'

'Get Millett into his saddle. If he's bleeding then do something to keep him on his horse until we reach town.'

Callow complied, and eventually pushed Millett into his saddle. Millett was only semi-conscious but managed to stay in leather, leaning heavily on his saddle horn. When they set out for Pike's Crossing, Burnett rode behind his captives. They travelled at a canter, and it was late afternoon when the town showed on the skyline.

Few people were on the street when they entered it, and a sigh escaped Burnett as he dismounted outside the law office and tethered his bay. He noticed that although the faces he had known ten years ago were different, the town looked as if it hadn't changed at all. He conducted his prisoners into the law office, and looked around critically as he approached the desk. A big man, wearing a sheriff's badge on his shirt front was seated at the desk, reading a newspaper.

The sheriff looked over the top of the newspaper and regarded Burnett and the two prisoners with narrowed brown eyes. He was fleshy rather than fat, and there were small wrinkles around his eyes. His weather-beaten black Stetson was pushed back off his forehead, revealing sparse, sandy-coloured hair. His long, narrow nose bulged about halfway along its length where it had been broken years before. He had long legs, which were stretched out under the desk and his boots showed scuff marks and the need of repair. He was wearing a dark brown store suit, a white shirt and a black string tie.

'What can I do for you, mister?' he growled in a rough voice. 'You're a stranger here. What's your business in town?' He noticed then that Millett was bleeding, and straightened in his chair. 'What happened to him?' he demanded in a sharper tone.

'I shot him. I'm Cal Burnett, Sheriff. I own the B7 ranch. I rode in there earlier, and these two came out of the brush. Millett was holding his rifle across his saddle, covering me, and I told him to point the gun elsewhere but he didn't, so when I saw his finger tighten on his trigger, I shot him.'

'The B7 ranch, huh?' Snark scratched his smooth chin. 'I always thought Lance Burnett owned the spread. When I heard he went missing some time ago, I asked a lot of questions around town but got no satisfactory answers. He never showed up again, and his body hasn't been found so I assumed he left the county. Now you've shown up, and you've made a bad start by shooting one of Grint's men.'

'These two had no right to be on B7 range. I was shocked to find the place had been burned. But I'm the legal owner. They accused me of trespassing, and I had heard that Grint ran my brother off and took over the spread.'

'Who told you that?' Snark pushed back his chair and got to his feet. He was tall — well over six feet, and wore a sagging cartridge belt containing a .45 pistol on his right hip. He leaned his hands on the desk top and his arms bent slightly at the elbows as he allowed his weight to rest on them. His eyes were like broken glass as he gazed at

Burnett. 'Are you making an accusation against Big G?'

'Hell, no! I don't even know Grint.'

'So what do you want?'

Burnett shook his head. 'All I want is to find out what's going on, and locate my brother.'

'You could get yourself in a lot of trouble if you're not careful. Amos Grint owns Big G, and he's not a man to take complaints about the way he runs his business. You better walk small until you get the lie of the land around here. I pride myself on running a law-abiding county, and I don't want you causing trouble. Your brother was a hell-raiser, and I reckon that's the reason why he disappeared. So you better watch your step. That's good advice, and I sure as hell hope you'll take it. You could be in trouble for shooting Millett. You better stick around town while I dig into this and get the rights of the shooting.'

'I'm not going anywhere until I've found out what happened to my brother and how come Big G took over my spread.' Burnett shrugged his wide shoulders.

'There's an account at the bank in your brother's name and the money for the sale of B7, less back taxes, was paid into it. Amos Grint paid good money for the spread, and if you wanta know more then you better see Blaine at the bank. Now you get out of here and make yourself scarce. I can't guarantee your safety if you go around asking fool questions. I'll talk to these two, and I'll want to see you later to talk it over.'

The street door banged and Burnett glanced over his shoulder to see a bull of a man standing on the threshold, dressed in range clothes and a red check shirt. Two gun-belts circled his waist, containing a pair .45 Colt Peacemakers in tied-down holsters. His hair was red and aggression showed in his pale blue eyes. His expression was surly; his massive body tense. A deputy star glinted on his chest. His manner was eager, as if he couldn't wait to start trouble.

'That's my deputy, Rufus Hoyle,' Snark said. 'You could ask him about your brother, although I doubt he can add anything to what I've already told you.'

'Who's this guy?' Hoyle demanded in a grating tone.

'He's Cal Burnett, Lance Burnett's brother,' Snark replied. 'He's asking what happened to his brother. I've told him what I know, which is precious little. Is there anything you can tell him, Rufe?'

'Only that Lance Burnett was a trouble-maker and gave us a lot of trouble. I reckon he's dead. He made enough enemies around here in his time, and was fool enough to pick on Grint and his outfit. I say good riddance to him!'

'It sounds to me that Grint picked on my brother,' Burnett declared. 'If what I heard is true then Grint ran him out and took over my ranch.'

18

'You're talking up trouble, mister!' Hoyle shrugged his shoulders. 'You better take note of what happened to your brother and pull your horns in.'

'What happened to my brother?' Burnett countered.

Hoyle came forward until he was within two feet of Burnett, who did not move. There was menace in the big deputy's manner. He thrust his chin forward belligerently and stared into Burnett's expressionless face with hostile, unblinking eyes.

'We don't know what happened to him.' Hoyle stressed each word as if talking to a child. 'It's obvious that something bad cropped up, because he disappeared, and he's been gone six months. That should tell you a lot, so don't come around here asking stupid questions. All you can do is ride out and forget about the ranch. There's nothing here for you, so cut your losses and make tracks.'

'If my brother was murdered then I'm gonna look for his killer,' Burnett said, shaking his head doggedly.

'Some men never learn.' Hoyle shook his head and clenched his ham-like hands. 'Do I got to spell it out for you?'

'I get your message,' Burnett said patiently. 'That's why I'll do my own looking around.' He stepped around Hoyle, intending to leave.

The big deputy cursed impatiently and reached for Burnett's left shoulder as he dropped his right hand to the butt of his right-hand gun. His impatience turned to surprise when Burnett slid out of distance before his hand could grasp him, but Hoyle followed the movement instinctively, stepping in close and pulling his gun in a fast draw. Burnett was turning towards him, and Hoyle was shocked to see that he was already holding his pistol, the black hole of the muzzle pointing steadily at his chest. Hoyle halted his movement, shock hitting him hard. He had not seen Burnett's draw; it had been so fast.

'Put your gun away,' Burnett said softly. 'I can't believe you'd use it against a law-abiding man.' He glanced at the motionless sheriff. 'What kind of law do you run around here? Is this an example of it?'

'Hoyle is eager to keep riff-raff out of the county, and perhaps he goes too far at times.' Snark shrugged. 'But that's not a bad fault in these violent days. So what are your plans? If you start nosing around the county you'll find bad trouble. Amos Grint runs a tough outfit, and he won't stand for hard cases coming in and throwing their weight around. Why don't you go to the bank and talk to Henry Blaine? Then ask questions around town about your brother and see what kind of feedback you get.'

Burnett nodded and holstered his gun with a slick movement. He stepped around Hoyle, who remained motionless, gun down at his side, and then paused. He turned to face Snark.

'When I came into town earlier, before riding out to B7,' he said, 'the stage coach showed up and the driver was yelling that he'd been held up and his guard was dead inside the coach. What was that all about?'

'Are you gonna stick your nose into that as well?' Hoyle demanded. 'That is none of your business, mister. We're taking care of it, so butt out.'

'I hope you'll do more about the holdup than you've done about my brother's disappearance,' Burnett replied, and left the office, heaving a sigh when he reached the boardwalk. He cast a glance around the wide street, saw the bank on the opposite sidewalk, and crossed to it, leading his horse.

It was the middle of the afternoon and the bank was quiet. Burnett tied his horse to a nearby hitch rail and entered the brick building. The teller was in shirt sleeves, sitting on a chair behind his grille, drowsy in the heat. He looked up when Burnett entered the big room, but showed no interest, and yawned as Burnett asked for the banker.

'That door over there in the back wall,' the clerk said. 'Just tap on it and Mr Blaine will call you in.'

Burnett rapped on the door and a sharp voice bade him enter. He walked into a large, comfortable office, paused to close the door at his back, and then looked at the small man seated at a desk across a corner of the room. Henry Blaine was in his middle-fifties, small and well dressed in a light blue suit. His face was pale and smooth, his expression serene. His eyes were brown, and filled with suspicion at the sight of a stranger. He got to his feet as Burnett crossed to the desk.

'How can I help you?' Blaine asked.

'I'm Cal Burnett. I've just arrived in town hoping to find my brother Lance at the B7 ranch, which I own, only to hear that the ranch has been sold and Lance disappeared six months ago.'

Blaine's expression did not change, but his mouth opened although no sound issued from his throat. He drew a deep breath, his mouth remaining open like a sagging gate with a broken hinge. He sat down heavily in his seat and gazed at Burnett as if experiencing a shock, and made a visible effort to regain his composure.

'I didn't know Lance Burnett had a brother,' he said unsteadily. 'But I didn't come to this town until long after the war ended and there's much I don't know about. You say you own the B7. Lance always talked as if the ranch belonged to him. He didn't manage the place at all well and spent the profits like there was no tomorrow, while making enemies wherever he went.'

'That sounds like my brother,' Burnett remarked. 'How did Grint get hold of my spread when I wasn't around to sign it away?'

'Are you saying it was done without your permission?'

'Yeah, I am. So what happened?'

Blaine sighed and placed his hands palm down on the desk. He looked at a spot some inches above Burnett's head when he continued.

'I didn't know Lance had left the county until Sheriff Snark came in to inquire if there was money in the ranch

24

account to pay the overdue taxes on B7. I checked the account and found it empty. The sheriff suggested that I put the ranch up for sale, pay the taxes, and put the remainder of the money from the sale into the account, which is what I did, although I had a feeling that your brother would not return.'

'What gave you that idea?'

Blaine shook his head angrily, as if memories were bothering him. 'I learned that Lance was seeing my daughter Susan and, when under his influence, she began to kick over the traces, I assumed that he was bad for her and spoke to him, and barred him from seeing her again. He took some persuading, but finally left, and we all went back to living our lives peacefully without him. He was not nice to know, and frankly I was relieved when he didn't show up again. If you want details of the legal side of the sale then you can talk to Murray Vine, the lawyer who handled it.'

'I'd like to talk to your daughter. She

might know where Lance went, and what was on his mind at the time of his leaving.'

'I'm afraid that's not possible.' Blaine shook his head. 'She left here when he disappeared, and went to stay with my family back East. I heard only last week that she has met a decent young man and is planning to marry him.'

Burnett nodded, aware that he would learn nothing helpful from Blaine.

'Thank you for your time,' he said. 'I'm sorry I troubled you.'

'It's no trouble. I hope you locate your brother.'

Burnett departed and paused on the boardwalk to look around. He saw Rufus Hoyle across the street and watched the deputy lumber into the general store. He spoke to a passing townsman, asking for the whereabouts of the lawyer's office. The man jerked a thumb to the right.

'Just along there,' he said. 'It's got a board over the doorway. The lawyer's name is Murray Vine.'

Burnett led his horse and went on, located the lawyer's office and entered. A young woman was seated at a desk in the outer office, and she looked up at Burnett's entrance.

'I'd like to see Mr Vine,' he said. 'I'm Cal Burnett. I used to own the B7 ranch.'

The girl nodded, got up from the desk and entered an inner office. Burnett glanced out at the street and noticed Hoyle standing in the doorway of the store, looking at the lawyer's office, his right hand on his gun butt. A rider appeared on the left, and stopped at the sidewalk where the deputy was standing. They began to talk, and Burnett shook his head when the rider glanced across at the lawyer's office too. Experience warned him to expect trouble from the big deputy.

'Mr Vine can see you now,' the girl said, emerging from the office.

Burnett thanked her and entered to find a tall, lean, smartly dressed man seated at a desk. He was handsome, with black hair, a smooth, tanned face, and alert brown eyes. He was around forty-five years old. He stood up and came around the desk with out-stretched hand, and Burnett shook hands with him.

'I'm Murray Vine, Mr Burnett. I'm pleased to meet you, although I must say that I am not surprised to see you. I sent a letter to the US marshal in Kansas City complaining about the lawlessness in this county, and received a reply informing me that US Deputy Marshal Burnett would be arriving in due course.'

'I'm recovering from injuries received in the line of duty,' Burnett said slowly. 'I'm practically back to normal, and as I own a ranch in the county and was coming here for a spell I was asked to look into your problems. But I've found some trouble of my own, and that's what I'd like to talk to you about before we get down to law business. It seems my ranch was sold to pay back taxes. My brother was managing B7 for me, and he couldn't have sold the ranch legally because he had no share in it. This is my first visit here in ten years, and I'm finding nothing but trouble.'

'What you say puts a different complexion on that business,' Vine mused. 'I handled the sale. I well remember your grandfather, and he told me that he had left the ranch to one grandson and nothing to the other. He said there was bad blood in the family. All the Burnett family were loyal to the Stars and Stripes except Lance, who fought with the Confederates during the war. It's a sad thing when families are split like that. It leaves mental wounds that can never heal.'

'That's all water under the bridge now,' Burnett said. 'Lance disappeared in mysterious circumstances six months ago. He's presumed to be dead, but his body hasn't been found. I suspect foul play, and I'm going to try to discover what happened to him. In the meantime I'd like to know my exact legal position — the ranch was sold out from under me. And what is the position of the man who bought B7 under those circumstances?'

'In view of what you tell me, if you can prove that Lance did not have the right to sell then you are still the legal owner. I acted as family lawyer for Sam Burnett and, if you wish, I'll check back and see what happened.'

'I'd be grateful if you would do that.'

'It will take me a couple of days to handle it. Will you be staying in town?'

'I'll rent a room in the hotel. Now perhaps you'll tell me why you wrote to the marshal in Kansas City.'

Vine shrugged. 'The local lawmen are inadequate. There are robberies and rustling taking place in the county and no one is ever arrested. The deputy sheriff, Rufus Hoyle, is a poor excuse for a lawman. He's a killer — has shot three men in cold blood since he pinned on a law badge; he claimed they were bad men breaking the law. The list of outrages against law-abiding folks grows longer and longer, and it's got to stop. Only last week a stranger came into town. He carelessly flashed a wad of money, and was robbed and killed in the night. His body was found in an alley. It's a scandal the way the law is operating.'

'Leave it to me,' Burnett said. 'I'll run an investigation along with my personal line of inquiry. Can you give me the names of anyone who has had a bad deal from the local law?'

'I'll think about that and come up with some names for you. But it will be difficult to find anyone willing to talk about what they've witnessed or experienced.'

Burnett nodded. 'I'll keep in touch with you. Between us we should be able to put down the men responsible for the trouble.'

Vine accompanied him to the door and they parted. Burnett left the office and paused to check the street. He saw Rufus Hoyle still standing in the doorway of the store. The rider he had been talking to had now dismounted and had tied his horse to a hitch rail. Both men watched Burnett intently as he crossed the street and headed for the hotel, leading his bay.

Burnett kept his right hand close to the butt of his holstered gun. He could smell trouble. He lengthened his stride to get to the entrance to the hotel before Hoyle and his companion could close on him, and wrapped his reins around a rail in front of the building. When he glanced over his shoulder towards the store he saw Hoyle and his companion coming fast towards him; Hoyle was moving like a mountain lion stalking its prey . . .

2

Burnett reached the door of the hotel, but paused when a voice called his name. He turned quickly to face Hoyle, his face expressionless, but he was ready to flow into action if Hoyle had a mind for it. To his surprise, the deputy was no longer on the sidewalk. It was the man whom Hoyle had spoken to outside the store who had come up to confront him.

'I'm Ryan Farrell,' he said. 'I ride for Tom Askew, who owns the Diamond TA ranch. Lance was a close friend of mine. Hoyle said I might be able to help you.'

'Where did Hoyle disappear to?' Burnett studied Farrell, who was short and fleshy, with blue eyes and sandy-coloured hair. His face had a pleasant look about it, as if he was fully satisfied with life. His range clothes were clean; a blue shirt, green neckerchief and faded blue denims. He smiled easily as he looked into Burnett's eyes.

'He dodged into an alley back there; said he needed to check on the two Big G riders you brought into town. I'm glad to know you, Cal.' Farrell held out his hand, and Burnett grasped it. 'I feel as if I already know you, the way Lance talked about you. He had a lot of trouble from Big G in the last weeks before he disappeared, and I wasn't too surprised when I heard he'd gone. He'd hinted about making a run for it because he thought his life was in danger.'

'I'd like to have a long talk to you,' Burnett said. 'If Lance was run out of here, or killed, then I'll want to face the men who are responsible and I'll welcome any help you can give me.'

'I'll buy you a drink and we can talk,' Farrell said. 'If anything bad happened to Lance then I wanta know, and I'll do something about it. Have you met Amos Grint yet?'

'Not yet. I'm looking forward to making his acquaintance.'

'Watch your step when he's around. He's a range wolf, and I believed Lance when he said Grint was trying to run him out.'

'You seemed to be pretty friendly with Hoyle,' Burnett observed.

'No.' Farrell shook his head, his face suddenly grim. 'I was surprised when he called me as I was passing the store. I know the kind of man he is. He pointed you out to me and told me you're Lance's brother. You'll need to watch out for Hoyle, especially when he's trying to be friendly.'

'I've got him pegged for what he is,' Burnett said. 'Let's go into the big saloon, huh?'

'No. Let's use Sim's bar along here. All the bad hats use the big saloon, which is owned by Mack Brown. I caught Brown out on the range some years ago; it looked like he was rustling.'

'And you let him get away with it?'

'Only because I was alone and he had a dozen riders with him. I reported what I saw when I came into town, but the sheriff didn't do anything about it. The next thing I knew, Brown had bought the saloon, and it's been a meeting place for all the hardcases in the county ever since.'

They went along the boardwalk to a small bar and entered. A couple of men were leaning on the bar talking to a tall, thin man behind it, who looked like a couple of boards clapped together. His face was pale and he looked ill, but he was smiling and his pale eyes were lively. He wore a white apron that was tied tightly around his slim waist and emphasized his bean-pole build. He looked up at their entrance and a welcoming smile came readily to his lips.

'Hi, Farrell, how you doing?' he greeted. 'What brings you into town in the middle of the week?'

'Heck, I thought this was a Saturday,' Farrell replied jocularly. 'What day is it?'

'Thursday. You must be in love if you don't know what day it is.'

'Meet Cal Burnett, Mike,' Farrell introduced. 'Cal, this is Mike Sim. He rode for Tom Askew until he couldn't sit a horse any more. Mike, do you remember Lance Burnett?'

'Sure I do. I often wonder what became of him.'

'Cal and Lance are brothers,' Farrell said.

Sim stuck out a thin hand and Burnett shook it. 'Pleased to meetcha,' Sim said. 'Have you seen Lance since he left here?'

'I haven't seen him in years,' Burnett replied. 'That's why I'm here. I want to know what happened to him. Was he getting trouble from Big G?'

'Let's have a couple of beers,' Farrell said. He slapped a silver coin on the bar and Sim turned away immediately. 'I'm sure Lance was in big trouble with Grint,' Farrell continued. 'He told me a lot. He was accosted by some of Grint's toughest men, here in town and on the range. They tried to bully him into leaving, and when that didn't have any effect they worked him over.'

Sim placed two glasses of beer on the bar. He was listening intently to what they were saying. Farrell picked up his glass and swallowed a quarter of its contents.

'I was out to B7 this morning,' Burnett said. 'Saw the place was burned down.' He went on to explain about his meeting with the two Big G riders and the action that followed.

Farrell almost choked on his beer. 'Did you kill Hank Millett?' he demanded.

Burnett shook his head. 'I brought both of them into town and handed them over to the law.'

'And Snark accepted your story?' Sim demanded.

'He didn't throw me in jail,' Burnett said.

'Hoyle is thick with Grint,' Farrell observed. 'I don't like it. They're up to something, you can bet.'

'Hoyle tried to get tough but looked down the barrel of my gun and changed his mind.' Burnett recalled the incident. 'I reckon I'll have trouble from him later.'

'You can bet your boots on it,' Farrell agreed.

'And Grint won't let the situation rest until he's faced me,' Burnett continued. 'I want to meet the man who burned down B7.'

'Lance might have done that,' Farrell said. 'I heard him say he'd rather burn the place than let Grint get his hands on it. If you can find Lance you'll get answers to most of the questions you're asking.'

'Are there any of Lance's B7 outfit still working around here?' Burnett asked.

'Hell, yes! I should have thought of that. There's Joe Denton, who's riding for Frank Swain out at Lazy S. I reckon Joe will know what happened on B7 up until the time Lance disappeared. I'll drop in on Denton and tell him you're in town. I reckon he could give you a lot of answers.'

'Thanks, I'd like to have a word with him. I'll ride out to Lazy S later. I need to get things moving fast. When Grint learns what I did to his two hard cases earlier he'll be on the prod for me.'

'I'll be riding back to the Diamond TA later,' Farrell said. 'I can side you for part of the way.'

'That's good. We can continue our talk then. I need to take a room at the hotel and settle in.' Burnett drank his beer and, as he turned to leave, Farrell stuck out his hand again and they shook warmly.

'See you later,' he said with a grin. 'I sure do hope we can pick up Lance's trail. It'd be good to set eyes on him again.'

Burnett left the bar and went along to the hotel. He was alert, and spotted Hoyle standing across the street in front of a gun shop talking to the gunsmith, who was wearing a long white apron and had a rifle in his hands — a short, rotund man with excess flesh on his body. He and the deputy were evidently discussing the long gun. But Hoyle was watching his surroundings, and he tensed when he spotted Burnett.

Burnett patted his bay before entering the hotel. He paused at the reception desk, pressed his thumb on a bell push, and a woman appeared in the doorway of an office behind the desk. Burnett touched the brim of his hat, and admired her as he asked for a room. She was not old; in her middle-twenties, and her tall, lithe figure was pleasant to look upon. She was blonde, with well-kept hair that was piled atop her head in tight curls, and she was beautiful, with an oval face and deep-set blue eyes that reminded Burnett of a summer sky.

'I'm Lorna Brett,' she said, pausing for him to reply. 'My father is William Brett, who owns the hotel.'

'Cal Burnett,' he replied, noting that there was no ring on her left hand. 'I don't know how long I'll be around, but I expect to be here at least a week.'

'You can have a room on a weekly basis. Would that suit you?'

'That will be fine.' He signed the register.

'Do you have any baggage?'

'It's on my horse, what there is of it. I'll fetch it in shortly. Would you have known my brother, Miss Brett? Lance Burnett. He bossed the B7 cattle ranch until about six months ago.'

She froze for a moment, her lips compressing, and then lifted a hand to her mouth and her expression returned to normal.

'So you're Lance's brother. He spoke of you a great deal, and how you were not here to back him when he needed help.' She broke off, shook her head, and then apologized. 'Forgive me. It was wrong of me to speak so. But Lance and I were good friends, and he was in real trouble before he went away.'

'Did he go away? Have you heard from him since he left?' Burnett's hopes rose as he awaited her answer, and dropped when she shook her head. A bleak mood slipped over him as he considered.

'I didn't know he had gone until some days after he left, and he didn't leave an address.' She took a key off a board behind the desk and held it out to him. 'Room number eight — up the stairs and the second door on the left.'

He took the key and their fingers touched. He started to turn away but felt reluctant to leave.

'Did Lance tell you what kind of trouble he was getting and who was causing it?'

'He didn't tell me anything. I heard the talk that was going around, but I couldn't believe the half of it.'

'Thanks.' Burnett knew the conversation was leading nowhere and turned away abruptly, but she called to him.

'I'd like you to know that although Lance didn't have many friends around here, I always believed in him. He worked hard out at B7, and it was a shame it was all for nothing. But he wasn't afraid of anyone, and stood his ground. The odds against him were too great — so he got out. I can tell you that Lance was very friendly with Susan Blaine, the banker's daughter. You could speak to her. She should be able to tell you something about his last days here.'

'I've already talked to Blaine. He told me his daughter went East when Lance left, and she won't be back.'

'He told you that?' Lorna Brett frowned. 'That was a strange thing for him to say! I spoke to Susan this morning. She often drops in for a chat when she's passing. As far I can remember, she has never been back East. Why did Blaine lie to you?'

He nodded slowly. 'I shall ask him when I see him again. I need to know if Lance is dead or alive. If he's dead then someone will pay for taking his life. Don't repeat our conversation to anyone. I need to catch Blaine unprepared when I see him again.'

'You might do better to talk to Susan without her father knowing.'

'Thanks for the information. I'll look her up. I'll get my gear off my horse and put it in my room, then I'll make a point of seeing Susan.'

He was thoughtful as he went out to his horse, wondering why Blaine should lie about his daughter. What was the banker trying to hide? He took his saddle-bags, blanket roll and rifle up to his room and then rode his horse to the livery barn. Bill Fray was standing in the doorway of his office, and he came forward hurriedly when he saw Burnett, who swung out of his saddle.

'I was hoping you'd show up again,' Fray said. 'A couple of riders came in about twenty minutes ago, and one of them asked for you by name. They ride for Amos Grint, and were loaded for bear. I wouldn't wanta be in your shoes this minute. It looks like the word is out on you. That's pretty quick, huh?'

'Describe them,' Burnett said. 'I'll need to recognize them.'

'Brent Weedon and Pete Sawtell. Weedon is a big man — wears black clothes, and has his pistol on the left. His black Stetson has a silver band on it. Sawtell is short and fat — wears a dark green shirt, and twin guns on crossed belts. They're Grint's toughest gunnies. When they ride into town, everyone runs for cover.'

'Where did they go when they left here?'

'Along the street. I saw Hoyle stop and talk to them outside the barber's shop. He sent them to Doc Willard's office, where Millett is. But Rafe Callow rode out of town about an hour ago like his tail was on fire. You had some trouble out at B7, I heard. You shouldn't have shot Millett!'

'I wish you'd told me that before,' Burnett said. 'I would have let Millett shoot me instead of defending myself.'

'This ain't the time for joking,' Fray said. 'Right now you should be looking for a hole to hide in until those two leave town again.'

'Hiding away ain't a part of my game,' Burnett said. 'I'll look them up and discover what they want.'

'First, you'd better see Ben Field, the undertaker, and tell him what kind of a funeral you'd like.'

'Take care of my horse.' Burnett thrust the reins into Fray's hands.

He left the livery man gazing after him and went back along the street, intending to confront Weedon and Sawtell. He checked his surroundings as he walked, and when he saw a man peer out of an alley just ahead, on the other side of the street, he stepped sideways into an opposite alley mouth; the shot fired at him from the alley missed him by a hair's breadth because of his instinctive movement. The bullet splintered the corner of the building beside him. He drew his pistol and craned forward, weapon lifting for action. He saw the figure easing forward, ready to shoot again, and triggered his Colt twice.

His first shot tore through the man's

hat, which was sent skittering into the air before dropping on to the sidewalk. His second shot passed through the space the man's head had occupied a moment before. Gun echoes drifted across the street as men dived for cover, and a dog barked frenziedly.

The man fled instantly, lost to sight in the alley. Burnett lunged forward, ran across the street, and peered into the alley the man was using. He was just in time to see a figure darting out of the far end where it connected with the back lots. The man turned to the left. Burnett exhaled sharply and lowered his gun, but followed quickly. He was breathing heavily when he reached the back lots and paused to look around. There was no sign of the man, and Burnett guessed he had run into another alley to regain the main street. He realized that it would be useless to continue the pursuit, but just then a gun fired at him from another alley. He saw a puff of gun smoke emerging from an alley mouth only yards away, heard the whine of a slug passing his right ear, and ran forward again, despite two more shots being fired at him.

He reached the alley in time to see the man running for the main street, and gave chase, firing a shot when the man stumbled and almost stopped. He fired again, and saw the man drop to his knees, then fall forward on to his face to remain motionless. Burnett went forward, his gun ready, and paused beside the still figure.

He was about to check the man when a harsh voice called his name. He turned quickly, gun lifting, but froze when he saw Rufus Hoyle standing on the sidewalk looking into the alley. The big deputy was holding a pistol, and cocked it when he took in the situation.

'Looks like I got you dead to rights, Burnett,' Hoyle rasped. 'You shot him in the back. It was cold-blooded murder.'

'Hold your horses,' Burnett said quickly. 'You saw the end of the shooting. It started when this guy took a shot at me across the street from another alley. He ambushed me.'

'You got anyone to back up your words?' Hoyle demanded. 'I don't see any witnesses.'

'We witnessed the ambush, Hoyle,' said a voice out of Burnett's sight, and two men stepped up beside the deputy. Burnett recognized them from the liveryman's description of them: Brent Weedon and Pete Sawtell, two of Amos Grint's top guns . . .

3

Bill Fray had described the Big G gun men accurately. Brent Weedon looked like an undertaker with his black jacket, trousers, and a black hat jammed on his head to complete the impression. He was very tall. His pale face was expressionless, yet managed to convey hostility. His brown eyes glinted with deadly intention. He gave an impression of a killer dog, straining at a leash — eager to tear human flesh to shreds. His hands were down at his sides as he faced Hoyle, but his jacket was tucked behind his holstered gun, and his right hand was tensed to make a play for the weapon should the need arise. The man with him was smaller. He had a grin on his fleshy face, and his right hand was resting on the butt of his holstered gun.

'You're Burnett,' Weedon said — a statement rather than a question — and he was looking at Burnett as he used his right hand to push Hoyle in the chest. Hoyle went backwards moving his feet quickly to maintain his balance. He recovered, but remained motionless, his gun hand down at his side, a smile on his face although his eyes were cold and filled with rage. Burnett frowned in surprise. He didn't think the deputy would back down from any man, but Hoyle was acting like a dog that recognized its master.

'I'm Cal Burnett,' Burnett agreed. 'You said you saw the ambush.'

'Yeah, that's right.' Weedon nodded. 'The ambusher is lying at your feet. His name is Jack Harmon. I thought I recognized him when he stuck his head out of the alley. If you have any more trouble with Hoyle then let me know.' He paused and glanced at the motionless deputy. 'Are you still here, Hoyle? Get the hell out while I talk business. If you want a statement from me about the shooting then see me later. Now clear out! My business with Burnett is more important than Harmon.'

'Sure,' Hoyle said. 'I'll come back when you've finished with Burnett.' He turned, holstered his gun, and walked away, a fixed smile on his fleshy face.

Burnett watched Hoyle depart, his surprise turning to amazement.

'I've been sent into town to escort you out to Big G,' Weedon said. 'Amos Grint wants to talk to you, and he ain't a man to be kept waiting.'

Burnett holstered his pistol. 'I plan to ride out to see Grint in the morning,' he said. 'Right now I want to learn why this man shot at me. You called him Jack Harmon. Who is he and where does he live?'

'Forget Harmon. You killed him, and that's the end of it.'

Burnett shook his head. 'I don't see it like that. Harmon ambushed me, and I want to know why. What's so urgent that Grint needs to see me right now?'

'I don't know his business, and that side of it doesn't concern me. Grint gave me orders, and I'll carry them out to the letter. That's how I work.'

'I don't work for Big G, and I've got other things to do right now.' Burnett shook his head. 'I've told you I'll ride out to Big G tomorrow, and I won't need an escort.'

'I hope this chore ain't gonna turn messy.' Weedon's face was expressionless but his tone was suddenly filled with menace. 'All you've got to do, Burnett, is ride with us and see Grint. That ain't such a big deal, is it?'

'You're the one making a big deal out of it.'

'But we don't frighten you, huh?' Sawtell cut in. His smile was gone and his expression showed belligerence; his eyes were bright with fury. The fingers of his right hand tapped the butt of his holstered gun. 'Do you figure to take us on? What's with you, anyway? All you've got to do is take a ride with us and see a man. After that we'll bring you back here. It's no big deal. There's no cause for digging your heels in and running the risk of getting shot.'

'Would you shoot me for standing my ground?' Burnett demanded. 'What kind of an outfit is Grint running? And why has he sent two big men to take me out to his ranch?'

'Like I said, we're only obeying orders.' Weedon thrust out his bottom lip. 'Don't make life more difficult than it has to be.'

'I ain't taking anything from him,' Sawtell rasped, his patience at an end. 'Who do you think you are, Burnett, trying to stand us off? You talk big, but can you back it up? I've finished pussy-footing around this. Weedon follows his orders to the letter, but I don't. Either you ride out with us or pull your gun.'

'Cut it out, Pete,' Weedon rapped. 'You heard what Grint said, or have I got to remind you? Fetch Burnett out here in one piece is the order, and that's the way it will be.'

'He's making fools out of us. We'll be the laughing stock of the county if you back off because he says so.' Sawtell stepped back a pace and held his right hand poised over the butt of his holstered gun. 'I'm calling your bluff, mister, so go to it. Make me back down.'

Burnett sighed. He glanced at Weedon's taut face, and Sawtell did the same, his attention momentarily diverted. Burnett pulled his pistol, his action setting off Sawtell as if the man was joined to him by the same mental processes. Sawtell jerked his right elbow and grasped the butt of his gun. The weapon cleared leather, but Sawtell stopped his action instinctively, for he found himself looking into the barrel of Burnett's steady gun.

Burnett did not fire — had no intention of doing so. He saw Sawtell's face express shock and smiled.

'You're a hard man to convince,' he said. 'How'd you manage to survive so long in your business?'

Weedon uttered a harsh laugh. 'He got you fair and square, Pete,' he observed. 'I'm always telling you not to go off half-cocked. Now do as you're told and stop playing games that might be the death of you.' He looked into Burnett's eyes. 'I'm taking your word that you'll ride out to Big G tomorrow. If you don't show up I'll have to come looking for you.'

'I said I'll be there, and I will.' Burnett nodded.

Weedon glanced down at the body on the ground. 'I'm wondering why Harmon set out to plug you,' he mused. 'Something is going on around town that I can't figure. You're treading on someone's toes, I reckon, and you'd better watch out. Don't treat Hoyle lightly. He's a killer hiding behind a law badge, and if there is something bad going on you can bet he's mixed up in it somewhere.'

Burnett holstered his gun, nodding. 'I've got my own opinion of Hoyle,' he said. 'I'll be at the Big G about noon tomorrow.'

'I'll tell Grint to expect you.' Weedon turned away, grasping Sawtell's shoulder and tugging him into motion.

Sawtell glanced back once at Burnett, and a stark thought crossed Burnett's mind — if looks could kill! They went back along the sidewalk, and Burnett stood watching them, a stream of impressions flooding his mind.

Before Burnett could move, Hoyle was back at his side, his grin back in place.

'Do you know Weedon from some place?' he demanded.

'Never saw him before any place. What about Harmon? How'd he get into this?'

'Why ask me? You were the one he was shooting at — you tell me.'

Burnett shook his head. 'It beats me,' he replied, looking down at the dead man. Harmon had not been handsome in life, and sudden death had put its own stamp on his thin features. His face was stiff, grey, and his sagging jaw gave the impression that he had been shocked and surprised when the fatal bullet struck him, like a deer that had been startled in a forest glade. 'Who is he?' he continued. 'What does he do around town?

'You know his name,' Hoyle said. 'And he's nobody around here. He never held down a regular job — fancied he was a fast gun, but he was nothing. He worked for anyone who would pay him, and most men didn't take him on twice because he never gave satisfaction. You say you don't know him. Did you know him when you lived around here?'

'I don't remember him, and his name is not familiar.'

'So why would a complete stranger want to shoot you?'

'That's what I'm asking myself, and the only answer I can come up with is that someone who does know me from the past paid him to kill me.'

'That's a thought that will cost you a lot of sleep.' Hoyle grinned. 'Weedon spoke up for you so you ain't got any charge to answer. You'll have to attend the inquest, but it ain't your business to find an answer to what was in

Harmon's mind when he ambushed you. I'll check him out.'

'Has he got any family in town?'

'No. He lived on and off at Ma Beeson's guest house. When he had no money for lodgings he slept rough, but even when he couldn't pay for a room he had money for whiskey. I reckon that's why he couldn't hold down a job for long — he drank too much.'

Burnett walked away, leaving Hoyle standing in the alley. He was surprised when Hoyle let him go without further comment. He saw Weedon and Sawtell entering the big saloon along the street and turned his face in the opposite direction, feeling the need to learn why Blaine, the banker, had lied about his daughter going back East. He went back to the livery barn, and Bill Fray looked down at him from the hay loft, a pitch fork in his hands.

'I heard the shooting a while back,' Fray said. 'It couldn't have been Weedon after you else you'd be dead.'

Burnett explained what had happened, and Fray leaned on his pitchfork and considered.

'Can you tell me anything about Harmon?' Burnett asked. 'I'd like to know why he tried to kill me.'

'If you don't know him then he must have done it for the money,' Fray mused. 'That's how he lived — thieving, rustling — and murder, no doubt. I saw him hanging around with Elroy Deke a couple of times, and that usually means trouble for someone. At one time, Deke worked for your brother out at B7, and you could do worse than talk to him about those days. He rides for Chuck Doan out at Circle D; he might know something that will help you get at the truth. But he's a shiftless sort, and can't hang on to a job. You didn't show up in town until this morning, and I suppose no one around here knew you were coming, huh? So how could anyone plan to ambush you? No, I reckon you walked into trouble when you showed up — trouble which started years ago. Someone has been waiting for you to return.'

Burnett's eyes glinted as he listened to Fray, for a sudden thought had struck him. He was thinking that someone in town knew of his coming: Murray Vine, the lawyer. Vine had contacted the US marshal in Dodge City to complain about local violence, and the marshal had furnished the information.

'I'll talk to you later, Bill,' he said. 'I've got a couple of things I need to check out.'

He turned away and walked to the big houses where the foremost towns-folk were located in a side street. The Blaine family lived in the biggest house, which stood apart from its neighbours. Burnett recalled Susan Blaine. He had always had a soft spot for her, and wondered how she had become involved with Lance. He knocked at the front door and waited for a reply. He spotted a movement in the curtains drawn across the front window. He was being observed. A moment later the door opened and Susan Blaine appeared before him. He recognized her instantly, and she recognized him.

'Cal Burnett, I do declare!' she exclaimed.

'Hi, Susan.' He blinked as he mentally discarded the old image of her as a gawky school girl and substituted the appearance of this beautiful woman. 'It's been a long time, but I would have known you anywhere.'

'And I wouldn't have passed you in the street if we had met,' she replied in a low tone. She was small, and had a lithe figure that was enhanced by the blue dress she was wearing. Her long hair was the colour of sun-ripened corn. He remembered her blue eyes, for they were vivid, depthless, shining now, as she showed her pleasure at seeing him. He was amazed by the fact that a thin, gangly child could grow into such a smooth-skinned, beautiful woman.

'Forgive me for dropping in on you

unexpectedly,' he said. 'I'm worried about Lance, and I heard that you and he had become friends just before he was run out six months ago. Do you know what happened to him?'

'Come in, Cal.' She moved out of the doorway as she spoke, and he took off his hat and entered a long hall that went right through the centre of the house to a back door. Her expression had become serious at the mention of his brother's name. She closed the door and led him into a sitting room that opened off the hall. 'I'm afraid Lance made a bad impression on my father before he left, so we must try to keep your visit secret. I had a lot of trouble because of Lance, and I wouldn't want to rake up any of that old business.'

'I'm sorry to hear that. I spoke to your father at the bank earlier and he told me something of what happened. He said you weren't around to talk to me. He told me you had gone back East.'

A shadow crossed her face and she shook her head. 'Lance asked me to marry him, and I agreed to before he was forced to leave. I'm sorry to say I haven't seen or heard anything from him since then. I don't know where he is or what he is doing.'

'It seems he disappeared completely when he pulled out.' Burnett shook his head. 'I've got a nasty feeling he's dead. He isn't the kind of man who would disappear and remain silent about it. Can you tell me anything about the trouble he was getting? I heard that Amos Grint was after B7, and I learned, when I saw your father, that the ranch was sold to pay back taxes and the remainder of the cash from the sale was put into the ranch account. I rode out to the spread and found it had been burned to the ground. And a short time ago I was approached by two of Grint's gun hands and asked to ride out to Big G with them.'

'You're not going!' Horror sounded in her voice as she shook her head.

'I'm riding out in the morning.' His tone was cold and determined.

'That could be a mistake, Cal.'

'I don't have any choice. If I don't go of my own free will those gun hands will be back to take me out. Anyway, I need to see Grint and find out what kind of a man he is.'

'I wish there was something I could tell you that would help, but Lance was pretty close-mouthed about what was happening to him, and no one around town tried to help him. I guess most folks were scared of Grint. He runs a very tough outfit, and they've got even worse lately.'

'I'll find out what's been going on.'

'There was bad blood between you and Lance,' she observed. 'He told me about it. He fought for the Rebels during the war and the rest of your family were for the Union.'

'It was something like that.' He nodded, keeping his mind from returning to the rut of bad thoughts about the way his family had been split right down the middle. 'I guess Lance had a right to fight for what he believed in. I saw him at the end of the war. He came back to the north and found it hard going. Folks around here didn't give him a chance. The job I went into when I left the cavalry didn't give me enough time to run B7, which came to me when my grandfather died, so I offered the job to Lance, and he took it.'

'He was doing all right until trouble broke out. Amos Grint took over Jack Peterson's ranch, bought out several adjoining spreads, and merged them to form Big G. That was where the trouble came from. Grint wanted B7 and couldn't lay his hands on it legally so he resorted to strong-arm tactics. He hired gun men, and then Lance disappeared and B7 went to Grint. They dressed it up so it looked like the spread was sold to pay back taxes, but Lance told me he had kept the ranch accounts up to date and didn't owe one red cent to anyone.'

'So it was a steal!' Burnett shook his head.

'I felt so sorry for Lance.' Her voice quivered. 'He was alone. The law couldn't or wouldn't help him. In fact Hoyle was down on him and made his life a misery. Lance talked about doing something about Hoyle, but he disappeared before he could get around to it.'

'I expect I shall have trouble trying to prove anything after all this time, but that won't stop me. If I have to turn this county upside down, I'll do it to get at the truth. Someone somewhere knows what happened, and I'll find him and make him spill the beans.'

'If what you suspect is true, Cal, the guilty men won't let you get away with it.' Susan shook his head. 'You'll disappear like Lance did.'

'That's a chance I'll have to take.' He nodded; his face grave. 'Lance never had a chance. He obviously didn't know what he was up against, but I do. If he's dead, he was killed fighting for my ranch; I'm not likely to forget that. Can you tell me anything about the bank robbery that happened before Lance disappeared?'

She caught her breath at his sudden change of subject, and for a moment she was uncertain. He noted her disquiet and wondered at it, but after an uneasy pause she moistened her lips and spoke normally.

'It was a bad business. Four men walked into the bank, killed Harold Smith, the teller who had worked for my father since the bank started, and escaped with more than $20,000. No one knew who the robbers were, and the money was never recovered. Of course, when Lance disappeared, everyone in town said he was responsible — had taken the money with him.'

'Did you see Lance after the bank robbery?'

'No. He was in town for several days, but I never caught up with him again.'

'Do you think he stole the bank money?'

'I don't. I got to know Lance pretty well, and he was not a thief.' She shook her head emphatically. 'The last time I did see him he was full of ideas for our future.'

Burnett twisted his hat around in his hands, suddenly impatient to leave.

'I won't call here again in case your father objects,' he said, 'but I hope I'll see you around town. If you do come up with anything about Lance after you've considered our conversation, then let me know.'

'You'll have to be very careful,' she warned. 'Someone is playing a deep game, and when he learns about your return you could be in the same kind of trouble that Lance faced. I want to help you, Cal, and if I learn anything that might be of use to you I'll tell Lorna Brett at the hotel, and she'll pass it on. She's a very good friend.'

He nodded, and was thoughtful as he departed. A pang of hunger struck him as he returned to Main Street, and he went immediately to Mike's Diner, which he remembered from before the war. But Mike Dennison was not there, and Burnett learned that he had retired five years before. He had a meal, and was drinking coffee when a man entered the diner, looked around, and came to his table. He was short and fleshy, wore a black beard that was liberally streaked with grey, and had a pair of brown eyes that overlooked a large hawk nose.

'Cal Burnett!' he declared, peering down at Burnett. 'I heard you were back in town.'

'Word travels fast around here,' Burnett commented. 'But you've got the better of me. I know your face but I can't put a name to it.'

'I'm Frankie Carver!' He said no more and waited for Burnett to react.

'Frankie!' Burnett nodded. 'I remember you from before the war. You were too sickly to enlist. My mother thought a lot of you, Frankie. Well, you're looking good now. What have you been doing since we said goodbye on the old B7?'

'With you and Lance gone to the war I stuck around to help run the place.'

'Sit down, Frankie, and let's talk. It's good to see a friendly face. So when did you leave B7?'

Carver dropped into a seat opposite Burnett and leaned his elbows on the table. 'When Lance took over as the boss I up and quit. I was used to old Sam's ways, but they didn't suit Lance. He made life tough for me so I left him to it. It was a hard decision to make, Cal, because I'd always felt like one of the Burnett family. I got a job here in town, helping Tom Jessup in his timber yard.'

'What happened to Lance, Frankie? Was he run out or did he quit?'

Carver leaned forward and gazed into Burnett's eyes. 'Cal, whatever else he was, Lance was no quitter. He was run out. I saw him here in town once, just before he disappeared. He'd been drinking, and was in low spirits. He talked to me instead of giving me the usual guff — belittling me and making fun of me. He must have been feeling lonely because he talked of the old times, and said he was sorry for a lot of things that happened. He wished you had come back because between you the trouble would have been settled in no time. I told him I'd help him any way I could but he shook his head. I never saw him again.'

Burnett suppressed a sigh. 'I didn't know what he was facing or I would have returned,' he said through his teeth. 'Did he mention who was giving him trouble?'

'I asked him that question and he told me it would be better if I didn't know. I'm real sorry, Cal, for not trying to do more.'

'You did the right thing by staying out of it, Frankie. I'm learning a few things about what was going on before Lance disappeared. Is there anything you can tell me that would help steer me in the direction of the men who were against Lance?'

Carver shook his head. 'There was a lot of talk at the time, and some pretty wild stories. But there was no way of knowing if there was any truth in them. Lance knew what was going on, and so did the men who were pushing him out.'

Burnett nodded. 'Thanks, Frankie. I guess I've got to do this the hard way. I'll see you around, huh? I've got to get moving. There are things to do.'

Carver got to his feet and held out his hand. Burnett arose and they shook hands. Carver preceded him out to the street and, as he turned to speak, a gun crashed from somewhere opposite. The slug struck Carver in the back and he was hurled forward by the impact, a cry forced from him. He collided with Burnett and they fell to the sidewalk. While Burnett tried to get clear of Carver a fusillade of shots hammered relentlessly, most of them smashing into Carver.

By the time Burnett got to his feet, gun in hand, the attack was over, and gunsmoke drifting on the breeze was all that remained as evidence — apart from Carver's lifeless body.

4

Burnett struggled with shock. A glance at Frankie Carver was sufficient to see that he was dead — struck by several bullets — and blood was draining from his lifeless body. Burnett forced himself into motion. He ran across the street and entered the alley between a butcher shop and the general store. The stink of gun smoke filled his nostrils and unaccustomed rage flared through him. He had been on the receiving end of the situation ever since he had ridden into town, and it was time he asserted himself. Being shot at from an alley was becoming a bad habit.

A man was leaving the far end of the alley, and Burnett caught a glimpse of a pale shirt that was not green or blue but a shade in between. He had seen it before: Pete Sawtell had been wearing it.

He ran to the back lots, and was in time to see the man hurrying into a barn some twenty yards from the rear of the big saloon. He ran in pursuit, gun in hand, aware that he was chasing Sawtell. He was still at a distance from the barn when a rider emerged and set off at a gallop across the open range. Burnett halted immediately and lifted his pistol; he aimed and fired. A moment later, Sawtell pitched sideways out of his saddle, hit the ground, and remained motionless.

The echoes of the shot scattered to the winds, fading slowly. Burnett went forward until he stood over the motionless figure. Sawtell's horse had halted a dozen yards away and was now grazing quietly. Sawtell was dead. Burnett's bullet had struck him between the shoulder blades. Burnett drew Sawtell's pistol from its holster and sniffed the barrel. It had been fired recently, and he was satisfied that he had got the man that killed Frankie Carver.

Several men were approaching from the rear of the big saloon, and Rufus Hoyle was leading them. The big deputy came to Burnett's side and bent over Sawtell, examined him and then straightened to gaze into Burnett's eyes.

'So what have you got to say about this?' He demanded.

'He ambushed me,' Burnett replied.

'Why did you shoot him in the back?'

'Because he was riding away.'

'Then it's murder. I'm arresting you, Burnett. There are witnesses to swear you did the shooting.'

'I've already admitted to shooting him — a felon escaping from the scene of a murder. It was probably me he was aiming at, but Carver got in the line of fire.'

'So you say.' Hoyle reached out his left hand and waggled his fingers. 'Hand over your gun.'

Burnett glanced at the five men who had accompanied Hoyle from the rear of the saloon, looking for Weedon, the other Big G gun hand. But he was not present, and Burnett did not know any of the others.

'Are you gonna resist arrest?' Hoyle demanded.

'So you can shoot me in front of witnesses? Not a chance.' Burnett grasped the butt of his holstered weapon with the index finger and thumb of his right hand and lifted it out of leather, keeping the muzzle pointing at the ground.

Hoyle snatched the pistol and stuck it in his waistband. He grinned. 'You know where the law office is,' he grated. 'Head for it, and don't try any tricks.'

Burnett set off immediately, returning to the alley and heading for Main Street. Hoyle followed him closely, breathing heavily.

'You're making a big mistake, Hoyle,' Burnett said. 'Why were you watching me around the street earlier? Were you expecting something like this to happen or were you waiting for your chance to shoot me? You've been against me from the moment you first saw me. So where do you stand in this crooked business?'

'You're talking through your hat,' Hoyle replied.

They reached the law office and Burnett thrust open the door and entered with Hoyle crowding him, prodding him with the muzzle of his pistol. Sheriff Snark was seated at his desk, looking as if he had not moved since Burnett left the office earlier.

'What's going on?' Snark demanded.

'I've got Burnett on a murder charge,' Hoyle replied. 'And there are witnesses. We can hang him legally.'

Snark leaned forward in his seat and picked up a paper from a pile on his cluttered desk. 'This is a wire from the US marshal in Kansas City, giving notice of a deputy marshal coming here. His name is Burnett. So stop playing games, Hoyle, and give him back his gun.'

Hoyle's grinning face changed expression until he looked as if the sky had fallen in on him. He gazed at Burnett as he tried to come to terms with the sheriff's words. 'You're a lawman?' he demanded.

Burnett reached into his jacket pocket, produced his shield-shaped law badge, and stuck it under Hoyle's nose. He reached out, took his pistol from Hoyle's waistband, and returned it to his holster.

'Why didn't you declare yourself when you were in earlier?' Snark demanded.

'That's the way it goes sometimes.' Burnett shrugged. 'You would have been told when I was good and ready. I'm not prepared to declare myself yet, so what is said in this office here and now will go no further until I feel the time is right to come into the open.'

'You have my word on it,' Snark said immediately. 'Let me know if there is anything I can do to help you. We're at your service.'

'What you can do is put a limit on Hoyle's activities. He's been following me around town like a hound dog. Make him the jailer; give him duties

that will keep him out of my hair
— stop him making a fool of himself.'

'Town jailer?' Hoyle said, frowning.
'We don't have any prisoners.'

'You will have shortly,' Burnett told
him.

'I'll keep him in check.' Snark nodded.
'What is it you're here to look into?'

'A number of things; one of them
being the disappearance of my brother,
Lance Burnett. But, before we go any
further, tell me what you know about
Amos Grint and Big G. I shot and
killed one of his gun hands — Pete
Sawtell, who ambushed me and killed
Frankie Carver. So what kind of a man
is Grint? He took over his ranch after
the war, so I have no knowledge of him.
Did he run my brother off B7?'

'The deal for your ranch was handled
according to the law,' Snark said. 'I told
you earlier to check with Blaine at the
bank.'

'I did, and it seems the sale was legal.
What happened when the bank was
robbed?'

'We investigated it and came up with nothing.' Snark shook his head. 'It wasn't a local job and no strangers were seen around town before it happened. My theory is that a gang moved in, made the steal, and departed afterwards. We never saw any sign of them.'

'And you've got no evidence that my brother was run out, huh?'

'It may look as if we haven't been doing our job properly,' Snark said heavily, 'but I can assure you that no efforts were spared during the investigation. I couldn't find anyone in town or on the range who saw your brother being troubled.'

'I'm riding out to Big G tomorrow morning,' Burnett said. 'Grint wants to see me. In view of the attack that was made against me by Sawtell, I don't want to take any chances. Get a posse together and trail me to Big G. I'll want you to stay out of sight but be ready to give me assistance if it looks like I've walked into trouble.'

'What time are you leaving? I'll have

a dozen men ready to ride, and we'll cover you every step of the way.'

'I told Weedon I'd be out there around noon, but I want to be at Big G around nine to keep surprise on my side. I was intending to remain incognito as long as possible, so let's play it my way. I'll ride into Big G as planned and face Grint. If I find trouble then you come in with the posse and arrest me for shooting Sawtell. Have you got that?'

'It'll be done as you say. You'll need to leave town about five to reach Big G around nine. You won't see us, but we'll be on your tail all the way.'

Burnett nodded and departed, leaving Hoyle scowling. He wondered if Snark could be trusted to do as he was told, and to keep Hoyle doing nothing but his duty. But he could do nothing more to protect himself, and was aware that just about anything he did on the morrow could go wrong. He went to the hotel and turned in. Night was darkening the sky, and it was time he drew his long day to a close . . .

He was on his way to the livery barn at first light, and found posse men already gathering there with the sheriff. He saddled his bay and rode out. The sun was above the skyline now, and he gave his mount its head. Four hours later he reined in on a ridge and looked down on the sprawling headquarters of Grint's Big G ranch. The house was two-storeyed, built of wood, and stood on a mound from which it overlooked everything. There were two corrals, three barns, a long, low bunkhouse located to the north, and several small buildings, including a cook shack.

Several men were in view, working the spread, doing everyday chores. Twenty or so horses were in one of the corrals and a dozen steers were penned in the other. The spread was obviously run efficiently, and no one was wasting time.

Burnett rode down to the gate, where a guard was standing, holding a rifle and looking alert. The man eyed Burnett suspiciously as he approached. Burnett reined in.

'You got business here?' the guard demanded.

'Grint is expecting me this morning.'

'You're Burnett.' It was a statement rather than a question. Burnett nodded. 'You're early. I was told you ain't due until around noon.'

'I'm an early bird. I don't suppose that will worry Grint.'

'Ride up to the house. Someone there will call the boss.'

Burnett rode through the gateway and crossed the hard pan of the yard. He could see a small man seated in a rocking chair on the front porch. The man was old — very old, and a younger man was sitting on the porch rail chatting to him. As he drew closer, Burnett could see the old man had only one leg, and his face was badly scarred. He reined up at the porch and sat motionless while he was regarded silently by both men.

'I'm Cal Burnett,' he said. 'I'm expected.'

'Not before noon,' said the younger man, who was dressed in working clothes but looked as if he did not do menial work. He was in his forties, powerfully built with wide shoulders and muscular arms. His pale blue eyes glinted as he regarded Burnett like something that had crawled out from under a rock. 'I'm Milt Candless, the ramrod. Mr Grint told me you'd be riding in around noon. Get down and wait here on the porch — talk to Billy. It'll make his day. I'll tell Mr Grint you're here.'

Burnett dismounted and tied his reins to a post. He stepped on to the porch and stood looking down at the one-legged man.

'Hi, Billy, you've got a fine view of the spread from here.'

'It was good a long time ago, but I'm tired of it now. I'm Billy Pitt. I worked on this spread before the war, and they carried me back here when the war was over. I was married to Grint's sister, but she upped and left when she saw the state I was in on my return. And I can't say as I blame her.' He laughed humourlessly, a dry, unemotional sound. 'I was blown up at Shiloh. That was one helluva fight.'

'I never saw one that wasn't bad,' Burnett observed. 'If you worked here before the war then you must have known Sam Burnett.'

'Old Sam? Yeah I knew him well. Looking at you, I guess you kinda remind me of him some.'

'He was my grandfather.'

'Have you seen what someone did to B7? Burned to the ground — there ain't two sticks standing. That was a bad business.'

'Billy, you talk too much,' a harsh voice cut in, and Burnett glanced over his shoulder to see a tall, lean man emerging from the house. He said: 'I'm Amos Grint, and you're Cal Burnett.' His pale eyes were bright, alert. He had a tight, mirthless smile on his rugged face. He wore a town suit of a smooth grey material, with a black string tie at his neck. His jacket was open and a cartridge belt showed around his waist. A pistol was holstered on his right hip. He looked hard, uncompromising, and aggression was evident in his manner. 'I knew you'd turn up one day, and I've been expecting you for a long time.'

'You sent two gun hands to fetch me in,' Burnett said sharply. 'I had the feeling I'd get shot if I refused.'

Grint showed his teeth in a quick grin. 'It's a tough country. You know now, I expect, that you don't own B7. I bought it when it came up for sale.'

'I heard about that.' Burnett nodded. 'But what bothers me more is the talk I heard about you running my brother out when he wouldn't sell B7. The ranch was left to me, and Lance was managing it while I was away. I'm checking up to see if the sale was legal because I wasn't around to sign the deal.'

'Pay me what I gave for it and you

can have it back.' Grint laughed when he saw surprise cross Burnett's face.

Burnett shook his head. 'The ranch was burned down. Without the buildings the place isn't worth more than half what you paid for it.'

'That had nothing to do with me. You'd have to talk to your brother to get the lowdown on that. He was a poor manager, and ran the spread into the ground. His crew deserted him and he finally ran out. You made a poor choice when you backed him.'

'So why did you send for me? Did you set Pete Sawtell on me? Do you know he's dead? Last evening he took some shots at me from an alley in town, and I killed him.'

'The hell you say!' Grint froze for a moment, his expression laced with shock. Then he turned to Candless, who was standing in the background. 'Did you know about Sawtell being killed?'

'No, boss. I'd have told you if I'd heard.'

'Find Weedon and get him here.' Grint recovered his poise and studied Burnett's face as Candless moved away. 'So you're a hellion, huh? Well you've made a big mistake coming here this morning if you did kill Sawtell.'

'It was self-defence. And you better know that I don't take kindly to threats.'

'So you fancy yourself against my outfit, huh? Do you reckon on shooting it out with the likes of Brent Weedon?'

'What did you want to see me about?' Burnett countered.

'To warn you against taking up where your brother left off. He raised hell against me before he went, and I ain't about to take any more trouble.'

'Did he leave of his own free will or did you run him out?'

'So you've been listening to the rumours, huh? Well get this straight. No one on my payroll lifted a hand against your brother. I went to the law when I got trouble, and Snark will be able to tell you what went on.'

'I won't take anyone's word.' Burnett shook his head. 'I'll check out my brother's disappearance and find out to my own satisfaction what really happened, and there'll be an accounting if he was killed or run out.'

Milt Candless returned, and Burnett saw Brent Weedon accompanying the ramrod. They came to the porch, grim-faced. Weedon held his left hand down at his side, close to the butt of his holstered gun.

'You killed Sawtell?' Weedon demanded.

Burnett explained the incident. Weedon listened intently and then shook his head.

'I told Pete before I left him in town not to face you again. I knew you'd turn up here this morning, but Pete disliked you on sight, and he was itching to have a go at you despite the order to get you here unharmed.'

'Is that all you've got to say, Weedon?' Grint demanded.

'You told me to get Burnett here in one piece,' Weedon said softly, 'and he's

92

standing before you right now. So what do you want from me? Have I followed your orders or haven't I?'

'Sawtell was your pard. You should be doing something to put the matter right.'

'I warned Pete yesterday to pull in his horns. What he did after that was his own business, and I'm not about to stick my nose in. If he shot at Burnett from cover then he got what he asked for. I fight my own battles, and that's that. If you want Burnett dead then do it yourself.'

'Am I hearing you right? You're supposed to do my fighting for me.'

Grint's expression grew sharper, and colour showed on his rugged features — a dull red flush that spread to his ears. He gazed at Burnett while he was talking to Weedon, and Burnett mentally steeled himself for action.

'I've done everything you asked me,' Weedon grimaced. 'Are you giving me orders now to do something about Burnett?'

'Don't talk about me as if I wasn't here,' Burnett said sharply. 'You wanted me to call, Grint, and so far I've heard nothing from you. If you've got anything to say then now's your chance to get it off your chest. I'm riding out shortly.'

'Do you expect me to order my men to shoot you?'

'Not while I can hear what you say.'

'I'm trying to stop trouble, not aggravate the situation. I tried talking to your brother before he left — not that it did any good.'

'So then you ordered your men to kill him. Is that how it happened?'

Grint shook his head. 'You'd better leave now, Burnett. We're just wasting our time. But before you go you should know that I'm being bothered by rustlers. If your brother is still around this range then I think he's involved in the steal. He obviously thought I ran him out, and he's trying to get his own back.'

'I don't know anything about rustling.' Burnett shook his head. 'And if my brother is still alive he wouldn't resort to stealing cattle. He's not a thief.'

Grint turned and walked back into the house. Burnett shrugged and stepped off the porch. He mounted his bay, and paused to look down at Weedon.

'What about Sawtell?' he asked. 'Have you got some unfinished business with me?'

'He asked for what he got.' Weedon shook his head. 'There's no need for me to step in against you. But don't come on Big G grass again.'

Burnett touched spurs to his mount and rode to the gate. The guard was standing in the gateway, rifle ready in his hands, but stepped aside just before Burnett reached him, and glowered as he passed him. Burnett heaved a long sigh of relief as he hit the open trail, his mind filled with questions.

Was Lance still alive? What had happened during the last days he was seen around? Why was Grint on the defensive? Was he losing cattle to rustlers?

A mile out from Big G the trail to town dropped into a low valley, and Burnett reined in sharply when he was suddenly surrounded by riders. He drew his pistol before he recognized Snark and Hoyle, and realized he had found the posse.

'Did Grint let you ride free?' Hoyle demanded.

'There was no shooting.' Burnet holstered his gun. 'You can take the posse back to town, Sheriff. I shan't need your help.'

'What are you gonna do now?' Snark demanded.

'I've got things to do. Thanks for your help. I'll drop in at your office when I come back to town.'

Snark nodded and turned his horse. The posse followed him in a close bunch as they rode out. Burnett sat his mount, considering his next action, and thoughts of his brother came to the forefront of his mind. He was no longer certain that Lance was dead. But what had happened to him, and where was he now?

He decided to visit Elroy Deke out at Circle D, and turned his horse to ride east. He hadn't travelled far when he got the feeling that he was being followed and, as soon as he crossed a ridge, he dismounted, trailed his reins, and crawled back to the crest to watch his back trail. He sighed sharply when Hoyle came into sight, obviously trailing him.

Burnett watched the big deputy for some moments, and then shook his head, went back to his horse, and continued. The sun was almost directly overhead when he finally sighted Chuck Doan's Circle D ranch, which looked deserted. There was no movement anywhere; no horses in the corral. He rode into the yard and reined up in front of the house. When he called he could hear his voice echoing across the yard. The small ranch looked rundown, but Burnett remembered Chuck Doan as a man who did nothing more than was necessary to keep the place running, and the fact that Doan employed a waster like Elroy Deke said a great deal about the rancher's character. He remembered Deke as no-good, shiftless, and unable to hold down a decent job. He wondered why his brother had associated with him.

He saw smoke issuing from the cook shack stove pipe and rode across the yard. The sound of the bay's hoofs on the hardpan brought a small man into the doorway of the shack. He took one look at Burnett, saw he was a stranger, and reached back through the doorway and picked up a Greener 12 gauge double-barrelled shotgun.

'It ain't healthy to ride in quiet-like,' the cook said. 'Who are you and what's your business? There ain't nobody here 'cept me, so what do you want?'

'I'm looking for Elroy Deke. I heard he works here. Who are you, mister?'

'Vic Reese, the cook.'

Reese was short and fat, in his

middle-fifties, and didn't look very clean for a cook. His black hair was long and greasy, his craggy face set in a scowl, and he looked as if he hadn't washed in a month. He was wearing an apron that had once been white but now was a dirty grey. He gripped the shotgun with claw-like hands, and looked as if he knew how to use it.

'What do you wanta see Deke about?' he demanded. 'He ain't here, mind you. Are you a lawman?'

'My brother used to go around with Deke some months ago. Maybe you know him — Lance Burnett. He was running the B7 until he disappeared. I heard he was getting trouble from Big G.'

Reese relaxed visibly. He lowered the shotgun and grinned. 'Sure I knew Lance Burnett — salt of the earth! Yeah, he was getting trouble from Grint. Deke was riding for B7 at the time. From what I heard, I don't think you'll see Lance again. I reckon he went down fighting and they buried him somewhere out on the range. You'll have a long wait to see Deke. The outfit are on a job and won't be back until after dark. Have you eaten? I've got some grub simmering on the stove. You're welcome to share it with me.'

'Thanks, I'd be pleased to.' Burnett dismounted and tied his bay to a corral rail.

Reese turned out to be a good cook, and Burnett complimented him as they finished the meal and drank coffee. Burnett had kept the conversation centred on his brother and the B7 ranch during the meal, but Reese either knew nothing of the subject or was not saying. As the cook got up to wash the dishes, Burnett heard hoofs outside in the yard.

'You've got company,' he said.

Reese hurried to the door, picking up his shotgun as he went outside.

Burnett got to his feet and crossed to the window over-looking the yard. Two riders were crossing the yard, approaching the cook shack, and one of them was slumped in his saddle, bleeding from a chest wound. Burnett went to the door and eased outside, his right hand down at his side, close to the butt of his gun. He recognized the uninjured man as Elroy Deke, and heard what Deke said as he stepped down from his saddle and turned to catch the injured man as he slid out of leather.

'There's been hell to pay, Cookie,' Deke said harshly. 'We walked into trouble. They were waiting for us, and cut loose as we went into the bank. Doan fell on the sidewalk; Meeson went down when the teller started shooting, and Jake got one in the chest as we jumped our horses and made a run for it. I don't think Jake's got a chance, but take a look at him. I'm gonna make a run for it because I reckon there'll be a posse on my back trail — '

He broke off when he caught sight of Burnett in the doorway of the cook shack, and reached for his holstered gun.

'Hold your fire, Deke,' Reese shouted. 'That's Cal Burnett, Lance's brother. He wants to talk to you about Lance.'

'The last time I saw Lance he told me his brother was a lawman!' Deke yelled.

Deke drew his gun and began to shoot at Burnett, and then all hell broke loose. Burnett dived back into the cook shack as Deke's first shot slammed into the door. He cocked his pistol, cursing his bad luck in turning up and catching Deke in a compromising situation.

Reese fired his shotgun into the door, shredding the woodwork. Burnett hurled himself through the back door, reluctant to kill Deke, and gun echoes hammered across the ranch.

5

Burnett tripped over a pile of trash outside the back door of the shack and went sprawling. He fell headlong, lost his gun, and rolled over. He could hear Deke shouting in the background and scrabbled for his gun, hunting for the weapon while keeping half an eye on the door. He felt the familiar shape of the pistol butt slide into his right hand and lifted the weapon as the door crashed open. Deke appeared, gun raised, smoking. He was shouting, although his words were more like animal sounds. Burnett lifted his gun into the aim, calling desperately.

'Hold it, Deke, I came here to talk to you about Lance.'

Deke brought his pistol to bear. Burnett's finger was trembling on his trigger. He waited until it was almost too late before he was satisfied that

Deke meant to shoot him. He aimed for Deke's right shoulder and fired. Deke jumped as if a horse had kicked him. He dropped his gun and fell to the ground, grovelling like a poleaxed pig. Gun echoes began to fade as Burnett went forward and snatched up Deke's pistol.

Reese appeared in the back doorway of the shack, minus his shotgun. He shook his head as he took in the scene.

'I'm only the cook here,' he said, raising his hands. 'I've got nothing to do with the robberies.'

'We'll talk later,' Burnett told him. 'Take a look at Deke. Patch him up. I want to talk to him.'

Reese came forward and bent over Deke. He looked up at Burnett with fear in his eyes.

'I can fix him up for a ride into town,' he said. 'But he'll need a doctor.'

'Get on with it. Who is the guy he brought in?'

'Jake Overfield. I'll look at him, but Deke said he didn't think he'd live.'

'What bank did they rob?' Burnett demanded.

Reese shrugged and shook his head.

'Come on!' Burnett rasped. 'You must have heard their plans.'

'They rode over to Prairieville and hit the bank there. They've been gone almost a week.'

'Get Deke ready to travel. I'll check Overfield.'

Burnett went through the shack and out the front door. He bent over the man lying beside one of the horses and discovered that he was dead. As he straightened he caught a movement to his left and swung round, reaching for his gun. He stopped the action when he recognized Rufus Hoyle walking towards him. The big deputy was grinning, holding his pistol with the muzzle pointing at the ground.

'I was passing and heard the shooting,' Hoyle said.

'What have you got here?'

'This outfit rode into Prairieville and tried to rob the bank. They were shot up. Deke brought Overfield back. Overfield is dead. I had to shoot Deke. He's out back, being tended by Reese, the cook.'

'Did they get away with any money?'

'I don't know yet. Take a look in their saddle-bags.'

Hoyle approached the horses and checked the saddle-bags. He lifted a cloth bag from one, and waved it, grinning.

'Looks like they pulled it off,' he said. 'They're probably the gang that robbed Blaine's bank in Pike's Crossing six months ago.'

'You're jumping to conclusions,' Burnett observed.

'There ain't too many bank raiders in the county,' Hoyle countered.

'Keep an eye on Reese,' Burnett said. 'I'll question him later. We'll head for town as soon as we can. Find a wagon and harness a couple of horses to it.'

'Where's Chuck Doan? I always reckoned he was a bad 'un.' Hoyle persisted.

'I haven't seen anyone else. Perhaps you'd better stick around here while I take Deke into town. Some of the others might turn up.'

'I'll wait,' Hoyle said. 'They might have some more dough on them.'

Burnett reloaded his gun and went back to Deke, who was unconscious. Reese had bandaged his shoulder.

'He'll make it to town,' Reese said. 'What are you gonna do with me?'

'I want you to drive Deke into town in a wagon. Rufus Hoyle has showed up — said he heard the shooting. He'll stay here for a spell in case any of the others show up.'

'I'll do like you say,' Reese said. 'As long as I don't have to stay here alone with Hoyle. He's got a bad reputation.'

Hoyle drove a buckboard around to the rear of the cook shack. He had thrown some straw in the back. Deke was lifted in. Reese sprang up into the driving seat and gathered the reins.

'Stick around here at least until tomorrow noon,' Burnett told Hoyle.

'I'll tell the sheriff you're here.'

Hoyle saw them off. Burnett mounted his bay and rode at the side of the wagon when Reese headed for the gate. They hit the town trail and made tracks. Burnett was thoughtful as they covered the weary miles to Pike's Crossing.

It was late evening before they saw the town, and lights were glimmering in some of the buildings fronting Main Street as they drove to the doctor's house.

'Stick close by me,' Burnett ordered Reese, 'and don't try to make a run for it.'

'I ain't broken any law,' Reese protested.

'I need to talk to you about the men who robbed that bank. I'll decide what to do with you later. Just don't give me any trouble. Get the doctor out here and we'll hand Deke over to him. Then I'll put you in a cell for the night and talk to you again tomorrow. When we talk you'd better tell me the truth about

108

your part in all this. Now fetch the doc.'

Shadows were filling the corners when Doc Willard emerged from his office. He was short and fleshy, with a rugged face and keen blue eyes.

'I'm Frank Willard, MD,' he said. 'I heard you were back in town, Burnett. I attended your brother, Lance, when he was shot just before he disappeared. Do you know where he went from here?'

'Not as yet, but I hope to get at the truth before much longer. We've got Elroy Deke in the wagon. I had to shoot him in the shoulder.'

Doc Willard hoisted his plump body into the wagon and examined the unconscious Deke.

'Let's get him inside so I can take a good look at him,' Willard said at length.

'He's a bank robber, Doc, so if you're gonna keep him in your place overnight then you'll need a guard to watch him. I'll get the sheriff to put a man on duty.'

They carried Deke into the doctor's office, put him on a couch, and waited until the doctor had carried out a thorough examination.

'You caught him slightly lower than the shoulder,' Willard said. 'I think you nicked his right lung. I'll operate and see what I can do. He won't be leaving here before morning, and he won't be in any condition to try and escape. I'll keep him sedated for twenty-four hours.'

'I'll drop by in the morning and see how he is,' Burnett said. 'Come on, Reese; let's get rid of the wagon.'

Reese drove the wagon to the rear of the livery barn and unhitched the team. Burnett rode his bay. Bill Fray appeared when they took the horses into the barn and was full of questions, but Burnett told him nothing, and he looked disappointed when Burnett departed, taking Reese with him. They walked along the street to the law office, where Sheriff Snark was seated at his desk, writing in a ledger.

Snark showed no emotion when Burnett explained what had occurred at the Circle D ranch. He picked up his cell keys, ushered Reese into the cells, and locked the door. When the sheriff returned to the office, Burnett was seated on a chair beside the desk. Snark lit the lamp on the desk before dropping into his seat.

'After you left me near Big G, I decided to ride to Circle D to talk to Deke about my brother,' Burnett said. 'I discovered Hoyle was trailing me, and he turned up at Circle D after the shooting. I told him to stay out there until tomorrow morning in case any of Doan's outfit shows up.'

Snark nodded his approval. 'I told Hoyle to keep an eye on you in case anyone from Big G decided to put you out of circulation,' he said. 'I'll have to ride over to Prairieville and find out what went on there. I reckon someone will ride in from there with a report. I've got a deputy there — Lew Chase. He's a go-ahead young man, and he's been on his toes ever since the bank here was raided. I'll do some more checking up on that, and maybe we'll tie Doan and his outfit to it. Does the doc want a guard on Deke?'

'He said no. Deke will be under sedation for twenty-four hours.'

Snark returned to his ledger and Burnett left the office. He was not feeling easy about Snark; when linked with Hoyle, the local law department seemed to leave much to be desired.

The street was shadowy when Burnett made his way to the hotel, but he was satisfied when he reviewed the day's events. His investigation was moving forward and, if he could get some witnesses to what had happened six months before he might even be able to clear up the mystery about Lance. Urgent questions surrounding his brother's disappearance niggled at his mind, and he was frustrated by his inability to make progress in that direction.

When Burnett entered the hotel he saw Lorna Brett at the reception desk, and she turned to him eagerly.

'Cal, Susan Blaine was here a short time ago. She asked me to tell you that she needs to talk to you about something that might help you. Would you call at her home as soon as you can?'

'Thank you.' He turned immediately. 'I'll see her now.'

Mindful of the attacks against him, he kept to the shadows as he made his way to the Blaine house. The area was peaceful, and lamps shone from many windows in the buildings he passed. He thought of his own home — blackened ruins that wiped out many memories of a previous family life — and his mind was filled with bitterness as he knocked on the Blaine door.

Susan Blaine opened the door to him, and he saw that she was greatly disturbed. She looked as if she had been crying. She clutched at his sleeve, drew him into the house and closed the door.

'What's wrong?' he demanded.

'I've had a terrible shock,' she said in

113

a faltering tone. 'Deputy Hoyle came, and I was so concerned by my father's manner at the sight of him that I eavesdropped on what Hoyle had to say. They went into my father's office. Hoyle had some news about a bank robbery in Prairieville. He was just at the Circle D ranch belonging to Chuck Doan — it seems that Doan and his outfit were the bank robbers, and Hoyle found something at the ranch which made him suspect that Doan and his gang were the ones who raided our bank here in town six months ago — and that my father paid Doan to do the robbery. My father went out with Hoyle. They were going to see a man called Carmby, who owns the gun shop along the main street. I also heard Hoyle say that he had shot your brother Lance, and mentioned a sum of money my father had paid him to do the shooting.'

'I saw Hoyle earlier, talking to the gunsmith,' Burnett said quickly. 'And I left him out at Doan's ranch in case any

114

of the outfit showed up from Prairieville. I'd better get after him. I didn't think he was much of a lawman when I first saw him, but from what you say he must be completely crooked.'

'What about my father?' Susan asked.

'If he's involved in the bad business that's been going on around here then he'll have to face the consequences. I'll come back and see you as soon as I can.'

Burnett left quickly and hurried along the street to the gun shop, which was in darkness, but lamplight shone from the window of the apartment above the shop, and he went into a side alley and mounted the external staircase. He could hear raised voices talking in the apartment. He drew his gun, and opened the door, then stepped quickly inside.

Hoyle was standing with his back to the door. Henry Blaine was sitting on a chair. He could see the door and watched Burnett's entry with shock spreading quickly over his pale features.

The gunsmith was standing beside Blaine, holding a pistol in his right hand and apparently threatening Blaine with it.

'Help me, Burnett,' Blaine shouted. 'They are going to kill me.'

Hoyle spun around quickly, his pistol rasping from its holster. Burnett knew there was no way of stopping the deputy except with a bullet, and fired a single shot that thudded into Hoyle's massive chest. Hoyle reared back as the slug hit him and struggled to maintain his balance. Burnett lunged forward and struck Hoyle's gun hand with the long barrel of his pistol. The gun fell from Hoyle's fingers. The big deputy fell heavily, and hit the floor with a crash that shook the apartment.

The gunsmith pointed his gun at Burnett, and then changed his mind and threw the weapon to the floor. He raised his hands. Blaine sprang up from his seat and came hurrying to Burnett's side.

'They were fixing to kill me,' Blaine

said in a quavering voice, badly shaken by his experience. He paused, gazing at Burnett, and his voice strengthened when he continued. 'How did you manage to walk in here at this particular moment?' he demanded. 'How did you know I was in trouble?'

'I'm after Hoyle,' Burnett said. 'Just stay quiet until I can get around to you; I've got some questions for you, Blaine.' He looked at the scared-looking gun-smith. 'You're Carmby, huh? Take a look at Hoyle and tell me if you think he'll live.'

Carmby bent over the deputy, who was unconscious, and shook his head as he straightened. 'I don't think he'll live through the night,' he opined.

'So let's get along to the jail and put you two in the cells. Then I'll get the doc to take a look at Hoyle. If either of you is armed then get rid of your guns now.'

Blaine dragged a .41 derringer from his right-hand pocket and threw it on the floor. Carmby shrugged and held out his empty hands. Burnett ushered them out of the apartment and down to the street.

'Get off the sidewalk and walk on the street,' Burnett directed. 'Head for the law office, and be very careful. I'm hair-triggered.'

They reached the office without incident and Burnett ushered them inside. Snark was not present. A small man was seated at the desk. He looked up quickly at their entrance, lifted a pistol from the desk as he arose, and covered them.

'What's going on?' he demanded. His dark eyes were beady, filled with suspicion.

'I'm Cal Burnett. Where's the sheriff?'

'He's off duty. I'm Seth Johnson, one of the night jailers. Snark told me about you, Burnett — you're a deputy marshal. So what gives?'

'Lock these two men in your cells and keep them here until I get back. I need to get the doctor over to Carmby's apartment to check on Hoyle. I had to shoot him.'

'You shot Hoyle — Deputy Hoyle?' Johnson demanded.

'I hope there isn't more than one Hoyle around here,' Burnett countered. 'Get moving. Hoyle is likely to bleed to death.'

Johnson holstered his pistol, picked up the cell keys, and led the way into the cell block. Burnett ushered Blaine and Carmby into adjoining cells and Johnson locked the doors.

'Don't let anyone in to see them before I get back,' Burnett said, and departed hurriedly.

He ran across the street to the doctor's house and hammered on the door. Willard appeared almost immediately, as if he had been waiting for a summons. Burnett explained the situation and the doctor picked up his medical bag.

They went quickly to the apartment over the gun shop and entered. Burnett halted on the threshold and looked around in surprise. There was blood on the floor but no sign of Rufus Hoyle.

'I thought you said Hoyle was dying,' Willard said.

'It looks as if someone exaggerated his condition,' Burnett replied. 'I'll organize a search for him, and call you if I find him alive.'

The doctor departed and Burnett looked around the apartment. He found a trail of blood on the floor and, with the aid of the lamp, traced it down the stairs and out to the back lots, where the trail vanished. Burnett returned the lamp to the apartment, locked the door, and returned to the law office.

'Is Hoyle dead?' Johnson demanded.

'Bring Carmby out here and I'll talk to him.' Burnett drew his gun and put it on the desk as he sat down.

Johnson ushered Carmby in from the cells and made him sit down facing Burnett across the desk. He stood behind the prisoner, a gun in his hand. Burnett regarded Carmby for a few moments before speaking.

'You're in a lot of trouble, Carmby,' he said at length.

'I don't see it like that,' Carmby replied. 'Blaine turned up at my place with Hoyle, and they bullied me. I don't know what they wanted, and Hoyle is a deputy sheriff.'

'When I walked into your apartment I saw you standing over Blaine with a pistol in your hand, obviously threatening him, and Blaine shouted that you were going to kill him. So why were you threatening him?

'I wasn't threatening him,' Carmby said sullenly. 'It was Hoyle doing all the talking. He told me to hold a gun on Blaine, and to shoot him if he didn't answer his questions. I held the gun but I wasn't going to shoot anyone. Ask Blaine. He'll tell you what happened.'

'Put him back in his cell and bring Blaine out here,' Burnett told Johnson.

Blaine seemed to have recovered his poise when he sat down in front of the desk. Burnett studied him silently for several moments, and Blaine became restless.

'Tell me what was going on when I walked into Carmby's apartment,' Burnett said at length.

'Nothing was going on,' said Blaine with a trace of defiance in his tone.

'When you saw me you shouted that they were going to kill you, and I saw Carmby threatening you with a gun. What was that about?'

'I was mistaken, I guess.' Blaine shook his head. 'Hoyle was there, and he's a deputy sheriff. Why would he want to kill me?'

'I wouldn't know, but I know when a man is covering up. Why did you go with Hoyle to see Carmby?'

'I didn't. Hoyle was there when I arrived.'

'That's a lie! Hoyle met you at your house and the two of you went together to see Carmby.'

'Who told you that?'

'I've been watching Hoyle's movements,' Burnett bluffed, not wanting to bring Susan Blaine into the situation. 'I followed him to your house, and then followed the pair of you to Carmby's.'

'There's nothing illegal in that, so why are you holding me?'

'Because you're lying, and when a man lies it's usually to cover up a crime.' Burnett glanced at the watchful Johnson. 'Put him back in his cell. He might feel more like talking in the morning.'

'You can't hold me! I want to see Murray Vine, the lawyer. He'll set you straight on this.'

'You can see him in the morning,' Burnett told him.

'My daughter will be worried if I don't return home tonight.'

'I'll tell her where you are. Lock him up, Johnson.'

Blaine protested all the way back to his cell, and Johnson was grinning when he returned to the office, jangling the cell keys.

'What do you reckon he's been getting up to?' Johnson said.

Burnett shrugged. 'I'm not in the business of guessing answers to questions like that. I'm going to look around town for Hoyle. I'll be back later.'

He left the office and stood in the shadows of a nearby alley while he considered what had occurred, but reached no conclusion and went back to Blaine's house. Susan Blaine seemed less agitated when she opened the door to him, but she was badly worried about her father, and looked at Burnett as if he was the bearer of bad news. When he had explained the situation to her she sank down on a couch and wept, her face buried in her hands. Burnett watched her in silence for some moments until, eventually, she recovered her poise and dried her eyes.

'I'm sorry, Cal,' she said. 'I've known for some time that my father has business worries. He's talked of moving away from here. Hoyle has something to do with it. He's always hanging around, and my father is usually in a bad mood after Hoyle's visits. Lately, it has been getting worse. I heard Hoyle shouting at Dad during one visit, threatening him, and a lawman shouldn't act like that.'

'Have you any idea what the trouble might be?'

She shook her head. 'Dad always denies anything is wrong.'

'He's probably got problems because of the bank raid.'

'Will you let him out of jail in the morning?'

'I'm only keeping him in there tonight for his own protection. Hoyle is wounded, but he's gone missing, and no one will be safe until he is behind bars. He's my priority now, so I'd better get moving and try to locate him.'

'Take care, Cal. He's a dangerous man.'

'I've got his measure.' Burnett departed, pausing outside the door until he heard Susan locking it. He went back to Main Street and, hearing music coming from the big saloon, headed in that direction, wondering where Hoyle might have gone. He looked over the batwings and studied the ornate interior of the saloon.

A long bar was situated along the right-hand wall, with three bartenders behind it and more than a dozen men leaning against it, drinking steadily. Ten gaming tables occupied most of the floor space, and they were crowded. A low stage was situated at the rear end of the big room, and a young woman wearing a red, low-cut dress, was singing, accompanied by a piano player.

Burnett studied the men at the bar, looking for Rufus Hoyle, but there was no sign of the deputy. He saw Ryan Farrell, the cowboy who rode for Tom Askew of the Diamond TA, standing at the far end of the bar, drinking beer and listening to the singer. Burnett pushed through the batwings and walked along the bar to where Farrell was standing. The singer finished her song at that moment and loud applause broke out.

'I'm on my way back to the spread,'

said Farrell with a grin when he saw Burnett. 'I just dropped in to hear Abbie sing. I've been sweet on her ever since our school days, although she's married now. Do you remember Abbie Fletcher, Cal?'

'Abbie Fletcher?' Burnett looked closely at the woman, and shook his head. 'The name sounds familiar but I can't place her.'

'At school she was a scrawny little bean pole with mousy brown hair.' Farrell laughed. 'We've all changed since then.' He raised his voice and called, 'Hey, Abbie, come and have a word with Cal Burnett.'

Abbie glanced in their direction, waved a hand, and then took a second look at Burnett, her expression changing. She pushed through the admirers surrounding her and came along the bar, a beautiful woman with glinting brown eyes and an attractive smile. She held out her hand when she arrived, and Burnett grasped and shook it warmly.

'I didn't recognize you when Ryan told me who you were,' Burnett said. 'It's been a long time, Abbie.'

'I didn't need to be told who you were,' she replied. 'I knew you the instant I spotted you. Where is that brother of yours? I was always sweet on Lance in the old days.'

'I'm trying to locate him.' Burnett's smile faded. 'I heard that he was in a lot of trouble before he disappeared.'

'I hope you'll find him in good health,' she replied. 'It's good to see you, Cal. I've got another song to sing right now, but I'd like to talk to you later, if you can stick around.'

'I'll be waiting here,' he said without hesitation, and she reached out and squeezed his hand before moving on.

'What have you got that I haven't got?' Farrell demanded, smiling. Then his smile disappeared. 'Do Abbie a favour and don't show any interest in her. She's married to the man who owns this place — Mack Brown, and he's a jealous cuss. He watches Abbie like a hawk.' Farrell glanced around, and then nodded. 'I thought so,' he continued. 'Here he comes now. He saw Abbie talking to us, and he's probably wondering who you are. Play it cool, Cal, for Abbie's sake.'

Burnett glanced to his right and saw a big man, immaculately dressed in a brown store suit, pushing his way through the drinkers, nodding to one or two as he passed them, but making straight for the spot where Burnett and Farrell were standing. He was dark-featured, with a sullen expression on his rugged face, and his brown eyes had a dangerous glint in their depths. He looked directly at Burnett as he approached, like a rattlesnake watching its prey, and Burnett felt a twinge of intuition as their gazes met for he sensed that Mack Brown was the most dangerous man he had seen in town since his arrival . . .

6

Mack Brown had a set smile on his face but it didn't fool Burnett. The saloon owner slapped Farrell on the back but his attention was on Burnett, and his voice was overloud when he spoke.

'You and Abbie looked like you were old friends,' he said. 'I'm Mack Brown. What's your handle?'

'He's Cal Burnett, Lance Burnett's brother,' Farrell said. 'You remember Lance, don't you?'

'I'll never forget him.' Mack Brown stuck out his right hand. 'I was about the only friend Lance had around here before he disappeared. In fact, I lent him two hundred dollars so he could make a run for it. His enemies had set him afoot and he had no place to hide.'

Burnett shook hands, and clenched his teeth when Brown exerted his strength and crushed his hand in a powerful grip. 'If you helped Lance when he was in trouble then I'm grateful to you,' he said. 'Do you have any idea where he went?'

'He went unseen in the night and kept right on going. What do you think of Abbie's singing?'

'She's good. I never knew she had it in her, but I haven't been home in ten years, and I've lost all contact with the folks I knew before the war. Who were my brother's enemies that you mentioned?'

'You don't have a home here now, so I heard.' Brown ignored the question. He was looking at the stage, where Abbie was talking to the pianist. 'I'll get back to you later, Burnett. I want to have a word with Abbie before she starts her next song.'

He departed and thrust his way through the throng at the bar, using his weight and strength to forge ahead. Farrell laughed harshly.

'You can see what kind of a man Mack Brown is,' he remarked. 'Take some advice from me, Cal, and don't get on the wrong side of him. And don't believe anything he says. He was never a friend to Lance. He's a jealous husband, and you don't have to go too far to arouse him. Ask any man around town who has looked twice at Abbie.'

Burnett nodded. He was watching Mack Brown and not liking what he saw.

'You said earlier that you once caught him rustling,' he mused. 'Whose cattle was he stealing?'

'It was Grint's brand.' Farrell picked up his glass of beer and drained it. 'I'd better start making tracks,' he said. 'I'll see you around, Cal. Watch your step.'

'You also said you reported Brown to Snark and nothing was done about it, huh?'

'Right on the nail! I don't know what you make of that, but I watched my back for a long time afterwards, and since then I've never said a word about other incidents I've witnessed around here.'

'We'll really have to get together for a long talk, Ryan. When are you coming to town again?'

'Not for a couple of weeks. But you know where you can find me if there's anything you want to talk over. I wish you luck in your search for Lance, but I think you're flogging a dead horse. You should have been around six months ago.'

'I wish I could turn back the clock,' Burnett said earnestly.

Farrell departed. Burnett heard Abbie sing her next song, and left the saloon just before she finished. He stood on the boardwalk, listening to the applause, and was thoughtful as he went back to the law office.

Snark was at his desk, talking earnestly to Murray Vine, the lawyer. He broke off when Burnett entered.

'Here's the man you need to talk to,' Snark said. 'He arrested Blaine.'

'I'm representing Henry Blaine, Marshal,' Vine said. 'What's the charge against him?'

'I'm holding him until the morning — protective custody,' Burnett said, and explained the circumstances of Blaine's arrest.

'I've talked to him and he's quite capable of handling his own security,' Vine said. 'The man who was threatening him is now in custody.'

'I think you should release him,' said Snark. 'Blaine is a well-respected member of the town council and needs to go about his civic duties. I'll keep an eye on him this evening and see him home safely later. Any time you want him you'll find him at the bank during the day.'

'Sure, turn him loose,' Burnett said. 'We'll keep Carmby behind bars. Has anyone reported sighting Hoyle?'

Snark shook his head. 'What was he doing at Carmby's when you shot him?'

'That's what I'd like to know. I'll continue looking for him. I'll check with the doctor now. Has Hoyle any known haunts around town? Where would he go with a slug in his chest?'

Snark shrugged. 'Your guess is as good as mine,' he declared.

Burnett departed and went to the doctor's house. Doc Willard was in his office, tending a youth with a badly cut hand.

'No,' Willard said when Burnett asked about Hoyle. 'I haven't seen him. Was he seriously wounded?'

'I thought he was at the time, but when I went back minutes later to pick him up he had got up and gone. I'll take a look around town. He's holed up somewhere, I guess.'

'You shot him?' Willard asked. 'But he's a deputy sheriff.'

'His badge doesn't make him bullet proof. He pulled his gun on me,' Burnett replied.

He went back to the street and walked through the shadows, thinking over the situation. He was getting nowhere, although there were men in town who had knowledge of the criminal activity going on. He turned in the direction of the livery barn, aware that in any town out West the man who really had his finger of the community pulse was the livery man. When he entered the barn he found Fray on the point of leaving.

'I won't keep you long,' Burnett said. 'There are just a few questions; one being about Rufus Hoyle. What can you tell me about his background? Where does he live? Is he married, or does he have a woman? Has he any friends in town?'

'There ain't a soul in town who knows much about Hoyle. He plays his cards close to his vest. He's got a room in Vera Gilchrist's boarding house on Main Street opposite the church. She runs a good place. There are a few men around town Hoyle keeps in with, but I wouldn't call them friends. He plays poker with several regulars, and I wonder why Henry Blaine associates with him. They ain't the kind of men to run together, but Hoyle is often at Blaine's house. There must be some connection between them, and it can't

136

be good, knowing the kind of man Hoyle is.'

'Cast your mind back to when my brother Lance was still around. Did he have a special friend in town?'

Fray shook his head. 'There were several women in his life, but with the men, he didn't have much success. His trouble was that he wore a grey coat during the war, while everyone around here was in blue. Is there anything else before I go home? I've had a long day.'

'Thanks, that will be all for now.'

Burnett turned away and went back along the street. He saw the Gilchrist guest house opposite the church and entered. Supper was over, and Mrs Gilchrist was cleaning the dining room. She was in her middle-fifties, well-fleshed, motherly. Her hair was grey and her lined face was gentle, sympathetic. She was short in stature, and was bustling around like a woman half her age. She paused in sweeping the floor when Burnett called her name, and smiled cheerily at him.

'If you're looking for a vacancy then I'm sorry to disappoint you,' she said. 'I'm full up.'

'I'm staying at the hotel,' Burnett replied. 'I want to talk to Rufus Hoyle, and I was told he lives here.'

Mrs Gilchrist's smile faltered and a shadow crossed her face. She sighed and shook her head. 'He's up in his room,' she said. 'I was coming out of the kitchen some time ago and caught a glimpse of him disappearing up the stairs. He didn't come down for supper, and I was about to take a tray up to him.'

'You can forget the tray,' Burnett told her. 'He's wanted at the jail.'

'His room is the first on the right at the top of the stairs.' She smiled and resumed her sweeping.

Burnett went up to Hoyle's room. He pressed an ear to the door panel and listened intently — heard nothing. Drawing his gun, he tried the handle with his left hand and the door opened. Burnett moved fast, lunging into the room, gun muzzle sweeping to cover the interior.

Hoyle was lying on a small bed — asleep. His shirt was open to the waist. A bullet wound was evident in the right upper chest, dribbling blood. Hoyle was unconscious, breathing heavily through his gaping mouth. His gun was in its holster, and Burnett took it and stuck it in his waistband.

'What happened to him?' Mrs Gilchrist appeared in the doorway with a tray in her hands. She stared at Hoyle. 'Is he dead?'

'Not yet.' Burnett turned to her. 'Would you fetch the doctor and bring him up here?'

She hurried away and clattered down the stairs. Burnett remained in the room, watching Hoyle until she returned some minutes later accompanied by Doc Willard.

'He's seriously hurt,' Willard observed. 'I'll need to get him into my office and start working on him. Stay with him until I get back with some help.'

Willard fetched three men and Hoyle was taken out. Burnett thought it was time to call it a day and headed for the hotel. Main Street was in heavy shadow, and a cool breeze was blowing in from the prairie. Apart from music coming from Brown's saloon, there was no noise. When a low whistle trilled across the street, Burnett heard it clearly, and sidestepped quickly into an alley mouth. He stood in dense shadow, gripping the butt of his holstered gun, his eyes strained to pierce the surrounding shadows. There was no movement across the street, but he did not discount the whistle. This could be a gun trap set up for someone, and he had been a popular target recently.

'Hey, Burnett, come out and show yourself.' The voice came out of the shadows across the street. 'I've got a bullet for you.'

Burnett drew his gun and held it ready. He could not identify the voice and waited, a pulse throbbing painfully in his throat. His gaze was centred on an alley almost opposite.

'The word is out on you, Burnett. You won't leave town alive. Come on out and I'll show myself.'

Burnett now recognized Weedon's voice, and tensed. He changed position, crouching as he crossed the alley mouth.

'I know it's you, Weedon,' he called. 'Have you got fresh orders about me? Does Grint want me dead now?'

'This has got nothing to do with Grint. I quit him this afternoon. I'm working for someone else now.'

'And that someone wants me dead? So why are you standing in the shadows instead of coming for me?'

'I wanta give you an even break. Step out into the open and we'll get this moving.'

'There's something you should know before we tangle, Weedon. I'm a lawman.'

'I reckoned on that when we first met. But that don't mean a thing. Come out of the alley and turn it loose!'

'I'm here for a special reason, and I don't get paid to dabble in gun fights. If you want me then show yourself and start shooting. I'll take it from there.'

He waited but there was no reply from across the street. Impatience plucked at his nerve and he heaved a sigh, turned on his heel and moved back along the alley to the back lot. Intense darkness surrounded him. He paused to allow his eyes to become accustomed to the black curtain that seemed to hang before them. When his pupils dilated and he could begin to make out details he went towards the rear of the law office.

He heard the sound of low voices conversing at the back of the jail and paused to listen. He could not understand what was being said, but wondered why two men would be out here. He drew his gun and crouched, pointing his pistol in the general direction of the sound.

'What's going on here?' he demanded harshly.

A gun blasted instantly, throwing a red-gold tongue of flame through the shadows. Burnett dropped to one knee as he called, and heard the slug pass over his head. He fired in return, and moved quickly to his left. Two guns blasted in unison, and as the echoes faded he heard running footsteps in the alley beside the jail.

He got to his feet and went in pursuit, throwing himself flat when crimson fire flared at the street end of the alley. A bullet struck something metallic within two feet of him and he lifted his gun and sent three spaced shots along the alley. He reloaded his gun while echoes rolled, and by the time silence returned there was no movement in the alley.

Burnett moved to the end of the alley and craned forward to check the street without presenting himself as a target. He was still motionless when he heard the door of the law office open and Snark's voice sounded.

'Is that you, Burnett?'

'How'd you know it's me?' Burnett replied.

'Nobody else is getting shot at around here since you showed up. What are you shooting at?'

'Whoever they are, they've gone now.' Burnett moved out of the alley and approached the open door of the office. The lamp inside had been extinguished. He made out the figure of the sheriff in the doorway. Snark was holding his pistol.

'Did you see anyone?' Snark asked.

'It was too dark.' Burnett shook his head. 'There were two men, and they were talking in voices pitched just above a whisper. When I challenged them they started shooting. You better check your prisoners.'

'They'll be safe. There's a yard along the length of the jail out back, with a ten foot wall around it. No one can get near the prisoners.'

'I was on my way to tell you that I got Hoyle. He's badly shot, and Doc Willard took him into his place. You can do what you like about him. I don't think he's well enough to make a break. I want him charged with attempting to kill me. How did he get to be a deputy? He doesn't seem to be the type, not by a long rope.'

Snark went back into the office and lit the lamp. Burnett followed him, closing the street door. Snark made no attempt to answer Burnett's question, and sat down at his desk.

'So tell me about Hoyle,' Burnett insisted.

'He came well recommended.'

'On whose say-so?'

'Murray Vine. It seems the lawyer knew him a long time ago. I needed a good man at the time so I gave him a chance.'

Burnett nodded. 'You turned Blaine loose?'

'Yeah, and Vine left with him.'

Burnett departed, and went along the street to Blaine's house. There was a light in a downstairs room, and Burnett knocked at the door. Susan Blaine opened the door and looked at him inquiringly.

'Sorry to trouble you but I need to talk to your father,' Burnett said.

'I haven't seen him since he left here with Rufus Hoyle.'

'Thanks. I'll talk to you later.' Burnett turned swiftly and hurried back to Main Street.

He reached Vine's office, saw a light in a downstairs room, and tried the door, which was locked. He knocked on the door and a moment later, Vine's voice answered.

'Who's there?'

'Cal Burnett. I need to talk to you.'

'Can't it wait until the morning?'

'Open the door, Vine.'

A bolt was withdrawn and the door opened a few inches. Vine peered out.

'What is it that can't wait until morning?' the lawyer demanded.

Burnett pushed the door and Vine was forced to step back. The door swung wide.

Burnett got a glimpse into the office

and saw Blaine seated at a desk. The banker was holding a glass of whiskey, and almost dropped it when his eyes met Burnett's.

'I thought I'd find Blaine here,' Burnett said. He entered the office and closed the door. 'I've got some questions for you, Vine, so sit down at your desk and pin your ears back.'

'The office is closed.' Vine shook his head. 'You'll have to come back tomorrow. I'm busy with a private client at the moment.'

'I've got some questions for your private client, but that can wait. It's you I want to talk to right now. You were the only man in town who knew my identity when I arrived. So how do you account for the fact that I've been shot at more than once? Who did you tell that Cal Burnett is a lawman?'

'I haven't told anyone! Did you force your way in to ask me that? If you leave now I'll overlook your action, otherwise I'll make a complaint to your office in Kansas City.'

'Don't try your lawyer stuff on me, Vine. You haven't seen anything yet.'

Burnett whipped up his clenched right hand and crashed his knuckles into the lawyer's face. Vine uttered a yell of pain and went over backwards, hitting the floor with a thud. He stayed down on his back, both hands to his face. Blood dribbled between his fingers and he began to choke. Burnett pulled him into a sitting position.

'Now let's get down to cases,' Burnett said.

He grasped Vine by the shoulders and dragged him upright. Vine sagged against him and Burnett braced him against the nearest wall.

'I'll have your law badge for this,' Vine gasped.

'Start talking, and tell me the truth,' Burnett insisted. He thrust Vine against the wall with considerable force, and Vine's head smacked the woodwork at his back. Burnett held him upright. 'I've been shot at from cover, damn

you!' he grated. 'I know you're responsible, so tell me about it before I beat it
out of you.'

He cocked his right fist and drew
back his arm. Vine watched him with
wavering gaze, his eyes watering pro-
fusely.

'Don't hit me again,' he pleaded.

'There's only one way you can get
me to stop.' Burnett threw a punch that
smacked against Vine's left eye. 'I can
keep this up all night,' he added. 'How
long can you take it?'

Vine's eyebrow split under the hard
knuckles and blood seeped into his
right eye.

'Stop,' he yelled. 'I'm not the one you
should be hitting. Blaine started the
trouble. He planned it. Talk to him and
leave me alone.'

A shot blasted, sounding thunderous
in the silence. The office shook. Vine
cried out and slumped into Burnett's
arms. Burnett looked up at Blaine,
seated at the desk, and saw the banker
holding a pistol with both hands, his

elbows resting on the desk top. Gun smoke was drifting around him.

'Put the gun down,' Burnett said in a steady tone. 'You won't help yourself with that.'

'Drop Vine and give me a clear shot at you,' Blaine replied. 'You two are the only ones who can give me trouble. I'm going to kill you, Burnett, and I'll tell the local law that you and Vine shot each other. Now drop him.'

Burnett supported Vine's limp body with his left arm and reached for his holstered pistol in a fast draw, his eyes fixed on Blaine. Blaine fired again, rocking the office with the report of the gun. Burnett concentrated on his shooting. He felt Vine jerk under the impact of a .45 slug as he thumbed back his hammer and aimed at Blaine. They were ten feet apart; Blaine saw Burnett's gun coming into action and was suddenly filled with desperation. He triggered his gun wildly.

Burnett fired once; saw Blaine drop the pistol as a bullet tore into his chest.

The banker reared up out of his seat, twisted, and then fell to the floor. Burnett released Vine's body. He stood for a moment before going to Blaine's side.

Blaine was still alive; blood stained his shirt around the right shoulder. He was unconscious, his face ashen with shock. Burnett picked up the discarded gun. The drawer in Vine's desk was open, and Burnett tossed the gun into it. He bent over Blaine to ascertain the extent of his wound, and decided that the banker was not going anywhere without being carried.

He left the office and stood on the sidewalk. Two men were coming towards him, no doubt attracted by the noise of the shooting.

'One of you can fetch the doc,' Burnett said. 'Tell him that one man is dead and another is shot bad. Make it quick.'

One of the pair set off at a run along the street. The other halted and looked at Burnett; could smell gun-smoke on him.

'Who is dead?' the man demanded.

'No names at this time,' Burnett replied. 'You'd better go about your business.'

The man stared at him, and then nodded and went on along the boardwalk. Burnett remained motionless, letting the night breeze blow the stink of the shooting off him. Several minutes passed before the doctor appeared, carrying his medical bag.

'Vine is dead,' Burnett reported as they entered the lawyer's office. 'Blaine is still breathing. I hope you can keep him alive. He's got a lot of talking to do.'

Doc Willard set down his bag and bent over Blaine. Burnett remained in the background, watching intently. After a couple of minutes, Doc Willard looked up and nodded.

'I think I can save him,' he said, and opened his bag. He plugged the bullet wound in Blaine's chest before getting to his feet. 'Stay with him until I get some help to move him,' he said, and went off along the sidewalk.

Burnett watched the doctor enter the saloon, and a moment later he returned with three men. Snark appeared from the direction of the law office as Blaine was picked up and carried to the doctor's house. He remained with Burnett outside the lawyer's office, and Burnett explained what had happened.

'You move fast!' Snark observed. 'What's next? Can I help you?'

'I don't know what's going on yet,' Burnett confessed. 'I'll make written reports about my law dealing when I can get around to the chore. At the moment I'm working in the dark, probing my suspicions based on observation. 'You'd better know that Weedon called me out a short time ago, along the street.'

'And you're still alive? Don't tell me you killed Weedon from an even break!'

'I turned down his offer. I'll have to face him some time before this is done,

153

I reckon, but it won't be on his terms. If Blaine is well enough to be jailed after the doc is done with him then watch him closely. He knows what's been going on around here.'

Snark nodded and departed. Burnett watched him stride back to his office, and when the sheriff disappeared into the shadows, Burnett went back to Blaine's house.

Susan Blaine opened the door to Burnett's knock, and looked frightened when she recognized him. Her hand went to her mouth and she suppressed a gasp.

'Has something happened to my father?' she asked in a faltering tone. 'I heard shooting some time ago.'

'Your father has been shot,' Burnett said in a low tone. 'He's alive, and the doctor thinks he'll survive. If you'd like to see him, I'll take you to Willard's house.'

'Who shot him?' she demanded.

'I did, to save my own life. I can't tell you more than that right now.'

'I won't go to him now,' she said. 'I expect the doctor will be busy with him for some time. I'll go to Willard's office later.'

Burnett nodded. She looked as if a strong wind would blow her over. He turned to leave her, and she closed the door very quickly on him. He moved into the nearby shadows and stood thinking. He saw the lamp in the downstairs room move, and a moment later it was carried into an upper bedroom. Susan was acting strangely, he thought. It could be shock, but he remained motionless; wondering what was in the girl's mind. Minutes later, the lamp came down to the front door, which opened. Susan emerged, paused to extinguish the lamp, and locked the front door behind her.

He eased deeper into the shadows as she passed him, and he could see well enough to note that she was now wearing riding clothes. She headed towards the stable, and Burnett followed, his interest and curiosity aroused. He remained in the background when she entered the stable, to reappear moments later leading a saddled horse.

Burnett watched her lead the horse towards the north trail before hurrying into the stable to prepare his bay for travel. Within a few moments he led the animal outside, swung into the saddle, and set out to follow the girl.

Out on the trail the night seemed less dark. A half-moon showed in a clear sky to the east, and range of vision enabled Burnett to see Susan's moving figure following the trail north. He eased off a little to his right in case she was watching her back trail, and continued without difficulty.

When she reached the fork in the trail that led to the blackened ruins of B7, Burnett was intrigued. He pressed a little closer, his mind alive with conjecture. The stark ruins of his former home appeared before them and Susan entered the yard and dismounted. Burnett halted in cover, tied his reins to the branch of a bush, and moved in on foot. When he reached the spot where Susan's horse was standing, he looked around in amazement.

There was no sign of the girl. He studied the shadow patterns across the yard, but she was gone as if she had departed for the moon. He made no sound as he edged through the shadows and approached the ruins of the house. The silence was heavy, like an unwanted blanket on a hot night. He kept his hand on his holstered gun as he stepped into the ruins, certain that he was alone in this ghostly spot for he could not hear any unnatural sounds, his senses telling him that there was no one around, and yet, as he ducked his head to pass through the derelict kitchen doorway to go and check the ruins of the barn, the muzzle of a pistol jabbed into his side and a harsh voice told him to raise his hands.

He swung quickly, hoping to take the man by surprise but, even as he moved, the pressure of the gun muzzle was removed from his lower ribs, and the next instant its solid barrel slammed across his forehead. He felt as if he had fallen into a bottomless pit where there was nothing but darkness, silence, and unconsciousness . . .

7

When Burnett regained consciousness, he remained quiet until his senses stirred. He had no idea where he was, and the only sensation he felt was a throbbing pain in his head. Dim light hurt his eyes, but he forced himself to look around. He saw a lantern standing on a shelf, and recalled that the B7 ranch was nothing more than blackened ruins. Had he been removed from the derelict cow spread? He remembered that he had followed Susan Blaine out from town, and that she had vanished by the time he reached the yard. He looked around, and winced at the pain evoked by the movement.

He appeared to be in a room that had earthen walls and, when he spotted a ladder to his right, a memory flared in his mind. This was the storm cellar in the floor of the kitchen of B7. The house had been burned down, but the cellar had apparently survived the fire. He lifted a hand to his face and gingerly felt around the large bruise that had swollen on his forehead. Dried blood crusted the bruise. He pressed both hands to his head and waited for the pain to diminish. Questions flared in his mind, and he pushed himself to his feet and staggered to the ladder.

The trapdoor above the ladder was open. Burnett forced himself to ascend, and when his head rose above the level of the ruined kitchen floor he spotted two figures standing together only yards away. One was Susan Blaine — the other a man who was embracing her.

Burnett reached for his holstered gun; found it missing. He remained motionless with just his head showing above the floor. His eyes became accustomed to the deceptive starlight and he gazed at the couple. The girl had her back to him, and the man's face was in shadow. Burnett strained his eyes to pick out details, but failed to recognize the man. With no gun, he was at a disadvantage, and his present position precluded action. He wondered why he had been put in the cellar.

He could hear the mumble of their voices, but could not make out what they were saying. His legs became strained on the ladder, and when he moved slightly to ease them the woodwork creaked. He froze, scarcely daring to breathe, and remained motionless, waiting to see if he had been heard. But the couple were intent on each other, and continued talking. He sighed with relief and waited, hoping for an opportunity to get to grips with the man.

Moments later, he heard a loud voice in the background, calling a challenge. The man whirled away from Susan instantly and began shooting into the shadows, moving several yards forward as he did so. Susan dropped to the ground and stayed there. Burnett sprang out of the cellar and threw himself down beside her. She pulled away from him as he placed a hand on her shoulder.

'Stay quiet and keep still,' he said in her ear. 'What's going on? Who is the man you're with?'

'It's your brother Lance,' she replied.

'Lance?' Burnett felt as if the world had stopped turning as he was overwhelmed by the news. 'If that's Lance,' he demanded, 'then why did he hit me?'

'He doesn't want you to know yet that he is around. He's got things to do.'

'And so have I!' Burnett got to one knee. Lance was off to the right, peering into the shadows, his gun uplifted, although the shooting had ceased. 'Lance,' he called. 'This is Cal. Give me a gun.'

'Stay out of this, Cal. I can handle it.'

Shooting erupted again, coming from three places beyond the spot where Lance was crouched. Lance returned fire, and one of the weapons immediately fell silent. Cal crawled to where

Lance was crouching. He grasped his brother's arm.

'Give me a gun,' he demanded.

Lance tried to shrug him off but Cal tightened his grip and the next instant his brother thrust a pistol into his hand.

'Have you any idea who is shooting at us?' Cal asked.

'Who else but Grint's outfit. The best thing you can do is take Susan with you and get the hell out of here. Take her back to town. I can handle this bunch.'

'I'm not leaving you now I've found you,' Cal rapped. 'I thought you were dead. I want to know what's going on around here, and where you've been for the last six months.'

'You always had to stick your nose into other people's business,' Lance laughed harshly. 'But this time you'll have to take a back seat.'

'No. You'll do as I say. I'm a deputy US marshal, and I've been sent in here to clean up. If I leave now then you'll accompany me, under arrest if that's the way you want it. Why did you hit me when I showed up?'

'Because I knew you'd do just what you're attempting right now. This is my business, Cal, and you'd better leave me here to handle it.'

'No dice! I'm not gonna argue with you, Lance. You'll do as I say.'

'You're asking for another crack on the head. Get out of here before more of Grint's crew show up. Where are you staying in town? I'll come and see you as soon as I'm able. Get Susan out of here. This is no place for her.'

'She came out here to meet you!'

Lance whirled to face Cal and thrust the muzzle of his pistol under Cal's nose.

'For God's sake do like I say,' he grated, 'before I overlook that you're my brother.'

'There are too many unanswered questions! I'm afraid that if I leave you now I won't see you again. I'm here on duty, and nothing can stand in the way of that.'

'I promise to come and talk to you as

soon as I can, and I'll be able to answer most of your questions.'

They both ducked when a fresh spate of shooting broke out. Slugs crackled around them and slammed into the blackened timbers over their heads. Cal glanced to where he had left Susan, and saw her flat on the ground with slugs striking around her position.

'I'll go,' he said reluctantly. 'Susan is in danger here. But you'd better show up in town soon and talk to me.'

Lance did not reply. He turned away and began shooting at the gun flashes stabbing at him through the shadows. Cal watched for a moment, and then crawled to Susan's side. He touched her arm and motioned for her to follow him, and then left the ruins. He circled around to the yard, motioned for Susan to remain in cover, and edged forward to fetch her horse. He saw gun flashes erupting from two spots off to his left, shooting into the rear of the ruins. Lance was replying with accurate fire. Cal grasped the reins of the girl's horse and led it away. When they drew clear of the yard he headed for the spot where he had left his bay.

He felt much easier when they were both mounted and riding back to town. The shooting behind them slowly fizzled out, and grim silence pressed in around them as they continued at a lope. His mind was inundated with questions, but he did not speak, and Susan was content to remain silent. When they reached Pike's Crossing it was early hours in the morning. They put their horses in the stable, and then Burnett escorted Susan to her home. When they stood at the front door, Susan finally spoke.

'I'm sorry for deceiving you, Cal. But Lance is living dangerously right now, and I can't do anything that might add to his troubles.'

'I'm his brother. How could it be wrong to tell me about his existence? I thought he was dead and felt terrible about it; and you knew he was alive.'

She shrugged. 'I did what I had to,'

she said softly. 'I love Lance, and I'll do anything to help him.'

'That's how I feel about him, so don't you think it would be better if we worked together?'

'I don't know what to think any more.' Her voice quivered, and when he looked at her he could see she was on the point of collapsing.

'I don't know about you,' he said, 'but I could do with some coffee.'

'Come in,' she said instantly. 'I'll make some.'

When they were seated in the kitchen, drinking coffee, Burnett heaved a sigh and shook his head.

'I don't want you to think that I haven't got Lance's best interests at heart. I'll do anything that's within the law to help him. But I have no idea what is going on around here, or what happened six months ago, before he disappeared.' He paused as a thought struck him, and then added: 'That's if he ever left the county.'

'He left,' she said instantly. 'He was

badly shot by Rufus Hoyle, and was near to death when I had him taken away.'

'Hoyle shot him? Why?'

'It was the night of the bank robbery. I had become suspicious of my father. He was acting strangely, talking to Hoyle and men like him — bad men — some of Grint's outfit, so I began to eavesdrop. What I learned made me think that my father was planning to have his own bank robbed by Hoyle and some of Grint's gun hands. Lance was having trouble at B7 at that time. Grint wanted him off the range so he could take over the ranch. I knew I couldn't talk to the local law because Hoyle was a deputy sheriff, and I suspected that Snark was involved. When I told Lance about what I'd overheard he helped me, and we discovered that my father was planning to have the bank robbed.'

'You could have gone to the prominent men of the community,' Burnett mused. 'But that is all in the past. When you heard Hoyle talking to your father about robbing the bank, did Hoyle agree to it?'

'He did, and also told my father that he could get the men to carry out the raid.'

'Would you give evidence in court about what you heard?'

'Yes, if it would help Lance.'

'Then I'll arrest Hoyle for bank robbery and try to get him to confess. This might be the breakthrough I'm looking for. Can I depend on you?'

'I'd give my life to help Lance,' she replied without hesitation.

Burnett got to his feet, and Susan arose.

'I must get moving,' he said. 'Keep quiet about what happened tonight. I'll come and see you again. Your evidence should tip the scales in my favour.'

He departed and went to Main Street. No lamps burned anywhere, and a chill breeze was blowing along the street. He went to the doctor's house, and paused when he saw a dim light in the office. He tapped at the street door, and a moment later it was opened by Doc Willard.

'I saw your light, Doc, so I thought I'd call. How is Rufus Hoyle?'

'Hoyle was taken out of here at gunpoint just before midnight,' Willard replied. 'I warned the men that moving him might kill him but they were not interested. They loaded him into a wagon and took him out of town. I reported the matter to Sheriff Snark, expecting him to do something about it, but he merely laughed. It seems he was pleased that Hoyle had been removed.'

'The three men who took Hoyle — did you know any of them?'

'I couldn't say for certain. They wore masks. But one of them looked like the man who brought in Millett, who you shot out at your burned ranch.'

'Callow,' Burnett said after a moment's thought. 'He's one of Grint's riders. Did you tell Snark about him?'

'No, I didn't. I waited for you.'

'Then don't tell anyone else or your

life could be in danger. I'll take it up now. Thanks, Doc. Now tell me about Blaine, and then I'll leave you in peace.'

'Blaine will make it, barring complications, but it will be a long job.'

'The men who took Hoyle didn't bother with Blaine?'

'They didn't see him while they were here, so perhaps they didn't know about him.'

'I'll arrange with Snark to have a couple of posse men in here as guards as soon as possible. I need to talk to Blaine at the earliest.'

'You can't talk to him for at least three days.' Willard shook his head. 'In fact I think it will be nearer a week before I could permit you to trouble him.'

'That's OK. I'll look in again tomorrow. Thanks for your help, Doc.'

He went on to the law office, where lamp light showed at the big front window. The street door was locked, and Burnett knocked. A voice challenged him from inside and he identified himself.

The door was opened a fraction and a bleary-eyed jailer peered at him, noted the law badge on Burnett's chest, and opened the door wide.

'I'm Al Kerry,' the jailer said, introducing himself. He was small, balding, and looked weighed down with the big Colt .45 holstered on his right hip. But his dark eyes were shrewd and alert. 'I was told to watch for you, Marshal. Sheriff Snark wants to see you as soon as you show up.'

'Where is he?'

'At home, I guess. He's got a house just this side of the livery barn. It's got a white picket fence in front of it. He said for you to call any time of the day or night.'

'Have you taken in any prisoners since you've been on duty?'

'No, and I was hoping to see Rufus Hoyle in here. They said you shot him. I'd liked to have seen that. Is he gonna live?'

'Doc Willard thinks so.' Burnett left and went back along the street. There

172

was lamp light in Snark's front window, and Burnett knocked at the door. Snark answered, and stepped back for Burnett to enter.

'What's on your mind, Sheriff?' Burnett asked, entering the house.

'I searched the town over for you earlier, and didn't see hide or hair of you. You should tell me where you are likely to be so I can contact you if needed.' Snark closed the door and led the way into a large room. He sat down in an easy chair, motioning for Burnett to seat himself opposite.

'I was out of town.' Burnett said, sitting on a leather-covered chair. 'Was there anything special you wanted to see me about?'

'Doc Willard came and told me some gunnies took Hoyle away. They're long gone now, but Willard said one of the men was Callow, who you brought in after you shot Millett.'

'I've talked to the doctor, and I'm riding out to Big G immediately to pick up Callow.'

'No need to look for me,' a voice said from a doorway behind Burnett, and a gun muzzle prodded him between the shoulder blades before he could turn. 'Don't turn around. I'm Rafe Callow, and I'll settle with you right now.'

Burnett was looking at Snark's face, and saw a smile appear on the sheriff's lips.

'This is the way it's got to be, Burnett,' Snark said. 'If I don't get rid of you now you'll get around to me in time. Me and Hoyle are running a gang in the county, and you've turned up to spoil our play so you've got to go.'

Callow snatched Burnett's pistol from its holster. 'Come on,' he said. 'Don't try anything. I'm not alone. Pete, keep him covered and don't take your eyes off him.'

'I'll plug him if he so much as blinks,' a voice growled. 'Millett was my pard.'

Burnett got to his feet and turned to face Callow and the man backing him. He recognized Callow. The man called Pete was tall and thin, with a hard face and cold brown eyes. Both men were holding pistols. Callow holstered his gun and produced a short length of rope. He bound Burnett's wrists behind his back.

'Take him out to Big G,' Snark said, 'and hold him there until I show up. Tell Grint I'll be out to see him in a couple of days.'

'OK, Burnett, let's get moving,' Callow said, 'and don't try anything.'

They left the house and Callow led the way to the livery barn, where three horses were tethered outside. They mounted and rode out of town. Burnett tried to loosen his bonds as they went on to the Big G ranch, but three hours later, as dawn was creeping into the sky, he was still trying to get free, without success.

The ranch was coming to life as they rode into the yard. Lamp light was showing in the bunkhouse, the cook shack, and the ranch house. Callow led the way across the yard and they dismounted in front of the porch. The front door of the house was open, and Callow called for Grint, who appeared.

'What's going on?' Grint demanded, coming out to the porch. 'What's he doing here?' he demanded when he saw Burnett. He cursed when Callow told him. 'I don't want him here,' he rasped. 'Why didn't Snark put him in jail?'

'Burnett is a deputy US marshal. He's already started cleaning up around town. He shot Hoyle.'

'I know that. Hoyle is here on the ranch, and I don't like it. I'm getting trouble from someone hanging around the old Burnett place. Two of the outfit were shot during the night when they dropped by there. Something is going on and I don't know what it is. Weedon quit cold on me yesterday.' Grint confronted Burnett and gazed into his eyes. 'So you're a lawman, huh? You tell me what's going on. What and who are you after? It better be the same man I want.'

Burnett shrugged his shoulders. 'If you've got trouble then you shouldn't mix with bad men,' he said.

Grint turned away. He grabbed Callow by the shirt front and shook him. 'You're making trouble for me, Callow, and I don't like it. Take Burnett back to Snark and tell him I don't want him here.'

'You'll be able to tell him yourself in a couple of days,' Callow said. 'Snark says he's gonna visit you. And don't give me a hard time. I'm only doing what I'm told.'

'Well I'm telling you to get him outa here. I don't wanta see him again. OK?'

'We could hold him for a couple of days,' Callow retorted. 'You know better than to go against the gang. They won't take that guff. If they ride in here on the war path, this place will finish up like B7.'

'Who burned B7?' Burnett demanded.

'Keep your mouth shut, Callow,' Grint snarled. 'You wanta tell the whole world what's going on around here?'

'Toe the line and there'll be no trouble,' Callow replied. 'We'll keep Burnett here a couple of days and that will be OK. Say, I've got a good idea. Why don't we put Hoyle and Burnett together? That might solve one of your problems.'

'I don't like Hoyle, but I put up with him because of who he is. OK, you can stick Burnett in where he can be locked up, and don't let him bust free. I don't have a spare gun hand to keep an eye on him so you'll have to watch him while he's here.'

Burnett, menaced by the gun Pete was holding, was led across the yard to the bunkhouse, which was now deserted.

'That's a spare bunk,' Callow said. 'Get on it, Burnett, and watch him, Pete, while I get something to tie him with.'

Burnett stretched out on the bunk under the watchful eye of his guard. Callow departed, and returned with a short length of chain which had a pair of manacles fixed to one end.

'Hoyle left this here when he brought that rustler in last year,' Callow

178

remarked, locking the manacles around one of Burnett's wrists. He passed the other end of the chain around the woodwork of the bunk and slipped the last link on the remaining manacle before locking it around Burnett's other wrist.

'That'll hold you.' Callow grinned. 'Now keep quiet. We don't wanta hear anything outa you before Snark gets here in a couple of days. Come on, Pete, let's get some grub.'

Both men departed, and Burnett tested the chain but soon gave up trying to get loose. He was securely anchored to the bunk. His only chance of escape would come when they released him from the manacles, and he had to be prepared to grasp any opportunity that might arise. He tried to relax, but his brain was teeming with the facts he had gleaned from Callow's conversation with Grint. He knew now where he had to push his investigation to get results, and impatience began to nibble at his mind as he considered the climax these lawless men would face.

His enforced inactivity gave him the chance to catch up on his loss of sleep. Despite his predicament, he slept until a foot crashed against the side of the bunk and disturbed him. He opened his eyes to find Callow standing beside him, holding a plate of food.

'You're a cool one,' Callow observed. 'How can you sleep knowing what's going to happen to you when Snark shows up? They can't let you live, knowing what you do. It'll be a lonely grave of the wide prairie for you.'

Burnett ate the meal, aware that he needed to maintain his strength for whatever efforts he would be forced to make upon himself if a chance to escape presented itself. Callow tested the chain, grunted his approval, and then departed, leaving Burnett to relax.

Presently, a tapping sound attracted Burnett's attention and he looked around curiously, trying to place the sound. He caught a movement at a window overlooking the rear of the bunkhouse, and saw a man peering in. His hopes soared when he recognized his brother. Lance was holding both hands around his eyes and against the glass to peer in, and he grinned when he saw Cal on the bunk. Cal lifted his manacles and waved his hands. Lance nodded and disappeared from the window. A moment later he entered the bunkhouse, gun in hand, and came to Cal's side.

'You've gotten yourself into a pretty poor state,' Lance observed. 'Did you see Susan safely back to town before getting yourself caught?'

'Get me outa here before we talk,' Cal told him. 'I've got this trouble pretty well sorted out. All I need to do now is get one step ahead of this bunch and I can clean up with some fast action.'

Lance examined the manacles and shook his head. 'You'll need a blacksmith to undo these without a key.'

'Lift the end of the bunk and free the chain and I'll be able to get off the bunk. I'll worry later about getting the cuffs off. Let's get out of here and then we can talk. I want to know what happened around here six months ago.'

Lance lifted a corner of the bunk and the chain, coiled twice around the leg of the bunk, fell free. Cal got to his feet.

'Have you got a spare gun?' he demanded, coiling the chain.

'I've got a couple of horses out back and there's a Winchester in my saddle boot. I saw them bring you in. I nailed one of those guys shooting at us at the old homestead and followed the other back here. When they brought you in I decided to stick around until the place quietened down before getting you out of here.'

'So let's get moving,' Cal said.

Lance led the way to the door, which opened just before he reached it. Callow entered, and halted in his tracks when he saw Lance. He started his hand to his gun butt, but froze when he saw Lance's pistol pointing at his belly.

'Where did you come from?' Callow

demanded. 'Half the outfit are out looking for you.'

Lance disarmed Callow and handed the pistol to Burnett.

'He put the key to the cuffs in his breast pocket,' Burnett said.

Lance found the key and unlocked the cuffs, and then locked them around Callow's wrists.

'If you know what's good for you I won't hear a sound out of you for the next fifteen minutes,' Lance said.

Callow nodded and sank down on the bunk Burnett had vacated.

'How many men are left on the ranch?' Burnett demanded.

'More than enough to get you and your brother,' Callow replied.

Lance grinned. 'I reckon we oughta raise a little hell around here before we leave,' he said. 'I've been on the wrong end of this business for too long.'

'Let's get out of here,' Burnett decided. 'I plan to come back with a big posse and clean up in good style.'

Lance nodded and pushed open the

bunkhouse door. Burnett followed his brother, and as soon as they were in the open a volley of shots hammered through the silence, forcing them to dive for cover as heavy echoes resounded and re-echoed across the ranch.

8

Lance hurled himself around the front corner of the bunkhouse with Cal in close attendance. When Lance dropped to the ground, Cal fell over him. Both whirled around and lifted their pistols. Lance was nearest to the corner. He stayed down and looked around the corner, thrust his right hand and gun into the open and began shooting at the men spaced out around the corral, all covering the bunkhouse. Slugs crackled into the wood work and splinters flew.

Cal moved quickly to the rear corner of the bunkhouse.

'Come on,' he yelled. 'Let's get out of here. Where are your horses?'

'At the back.' Lance fired several shots and then withdrew from the corner.

They ran around the back and Cal saw two horses waiting. He permitted

185

Lance to pass him, and when his brother sprang into the saddle of a sorrel he picked up the trailing reins of a black horse and swung into the saddle. As they galloped away from the shack, shooting came at them from a corner of the bunkhouse. Burnett whirled in his saddle and returned fire. A man standing at the corner dropped his gun, pressed a hand to his chest, and fell to the ground.

Lance set the pace and the direction, and they left the ranch hurriedly. More shots came at them but neither was touched, and eventually they drew out of range and were lost to view in a stand of trees. They passed through the trees and ascended to a bare ridge and reined in. Lance checked their back trail. He saw three riders emerging from the trees and following their trail at a gallop.

'We've still got company,' he remarked.

'I'm not running,' Burnett decided. 'Grint's outfit are ready to shoot anyone who crosses their trail, and he's mixed up in some crooked business, so I'm going to start law dealing. But I don't wanta lose sight of you now I've found you, Lance. I want to sort out the trouble that existed here six months ago, and you're the only one who can tell me about it.'

'I can tell you that in a few words.' Lance grimaced, his gaze intent on the approaching riders. 'Grint wanted B7, and he was prepared to go all the way to get it. I stalled as long as I could, but then the bank was robbed and the word went out that I stole the money. But I knew the robbery was handled by Snark and Hoyle, who were running a gang when they weren't acting like lawmen. Grint set Hoyle on to me and we exchanged shots. I wounded Hoyle — it was a pity I didn't kill him — and that was when I decided to pull out. But I was caught at B7 by some of Grint's outfit before I could get clear, and they set fire to the house to get me out. I was badly wounded and hid in the storm cellar until the fire died down. I took out when Grint's men left and made it to town. Susan got me away. I came back from Kansas City several days ago to carry on where I left off, and ran into you last night.'

'You didn't have to try and crack my skull.'

Lance laughed. 'I figured I owed you that. It's your ranch, after all, and I took all that trouble on the chin while you were away enjoying yourself.'

Burnett drew the Winchester out of the scabbard on the black and checked it. The three riders were drawing within range. He jacked a shell into the breech.

'We'll talk some more later on,' he said.

'I'll ride with you, Cal,' Lance said. 'I want to see how this winds up.' He drew his pistol and cocked it. 'Let's bring some law and order back to the range, huh?'

When the riders had drawn closer, Burnett lifted the rifle into the aim and fired at the nearest of the trio. The man vacated his saddle, hit the ground hard, and remained motionless while his horse ran on. Lance cut loose with his pistol, and a second man was dismounted. The third man wheeled his horse, withdrew hurriedly, and kept going even when he was out of gunshot.

Burnett looked around, searching the wide spaces adjoining their cover. He spotted some movement off to the right, and made out seven riders coming over a ridge, no doubt attracted by the shooting. They pushed their horses into a run and rode hell for leather along the trail that Burnett and Lance were leaving.

'There are more of them,' Burnett observed.

Lance gazed at the approaching riders and his face took on a resolute expression. 'I can see Rio Hotchkiss among them,' he declared, 'and Trig Hamblin. With Weedon gone from the Big G, those two are Grint's top guns. I saw them ride out earlier, and I was close enough to Grint to hear the orders he gave that bunch. They have to hunt me down and kill me if it takes them all week. We'd better make tracks out of here, Cal, or we'll be bogged down in gun hands all striving to earn the hundred bucks Grint promised to pay for my death.'

Burnett nodded. 'Let's ride,' he agreed. 'We'll pull clear if we can, and I'll have to work out a plan that will take care of these gun men. I can't go to Snark for help because he's working against the law. Come on, hit the trail, Lance, before we leave it too late.'

'You'd better follow me,' Lance replied, swinging into his saddle. 'I know my way around these parts. We'll lose them easily if we can pass them and head west.'

They moved out, and Burnett pulled in behind his brother. Lance stayed beyond the ridge, following a game trail that meandered in the direction he wished to take. They lost sight of the group of riders, rode down a slope and along a short valley, and then ascended another slope. Presently they reached a wide trail, and Lance reined in to check their surroundings.

'I don't think they know where we are,' he said, and ducked when a bullet crackled by his head.

'You're wrong,' Burnett replied as he spurred his mount over the crest of the slope.

'Now you tell me!' Lance retorted. They plunged down off the ridge and rode into more trees.

They descended to flat range land, and moved at a gallop out to the west. Burnett looked around to get his bearings. He followed Lance easily, content to let his brother lead. When they halted briefly, Lance dismounted and stood watching the approaches.

'I've been thinking about this business, Cal,' he said. 'I'm heading back to town as soon as I think it's safe to swing in that direction. You've got to nail Snark and the crooks in town before thinking of tangling with Grint's outfit.'

'That's the way I'm thinking.' Burnett nodded. 'Clean up the town and secure a good base, and then challenge all-comers. There are a lot of loose ends in this business, but a methodical approach will tie them up. I feel sorry for Susan because her father is a crook, and she must be aware of that now.'

'I'm gonna help her if it's at all possible,' Lance said. 'She saved my life six months ago, Cal, and I'll marry her when this business is over, if she'll have me.'

'We'll do what we can,' Burnett promised.

They went on, and Lance guided them in the general direction of Pike's Crossing, but they were still many miles from the town when evening shadows began to fall on the range.

'We'll have to keep moving,' Lance said. 'We got no supplies with us, and I'm getting ready for supper.'

'We'll hit town in a couple of hours.' Burnett replied. 'It'll be full dark by then, and I reckon to pick up Snark first. The rest should be easy, if done in stages. After that I can work on Grint and his bunch.'

'You'll know what to charge Grint with,' Lance said as they continued. 'He stole B7 from you, and I've got witnesses to prove it.'

The lights of the town were twinkling in the distance when they eventually topped a low ridge and reined in.

'This is where it starts in earnest,' Burnett said. 'Let's make for the back of the diner and get some grub, huh?'

They continued, and rode to the back lots on the east side of the town, dismounting in shadows and leaving their mounts in the corral at the stable. They walked through darkness to the rear of the diner. The kitchen staff were busy, and hardly looked up when Burnett led his brother inside. A waitress entered from the dining room with an order, and came to them as Lance closed the door.

'If you want supper, follow me,' she said. 'I'll get you seated.'

'I need to remain out of sight,' Burnett said. He indicated a table by a wall. 'We'll sit here, if you don't mind.'

'Only members of the staff are permitted to sit in here,' she replied.

Burnett produced his law badge and pinned it to his shirt. The waitress gazed at it for a moment and then nodded.

'I guess that makes a difference,' she said, and smiled. 'Sit down. I'll be with you in a moment.'

'Don't mention our presence to anyone,' Lance said, 'and tell us if Snark shows up.'

They ate a meal in silence and, as they were finishing, the waitress came in and approached their table.

'Sheriff Snark has just come in,' she said.

Burnett got to his feet instantly. 'I'll pick him up and jail him. You stay here, Lance, and I'll come back to you later. Lend me your pistol.'

Lance nodded and handed over his Colt. Burnett slid the weapon into his holster and entered the dining room. He saw Snark seated at a table by the door and crossed to him, drawing his gun as he did so. Snark looked up when he became aware of Burnett's looming presence. His jaw dropped in shock, and then he sprang to his feet, almost overturning the table in his haste. His right hand flashed to the butt of his gun, but Burnett's sharp voice halted his movement.

'If you pull your gun I'll kill you.'

Snark raised his hands and Burnett reached forward and relieved him of the pistol.

'Let's make for the jail,' Burnett said.

Snark turned and left the diner with Burnett at his heels. As Burnett closed the door of the diner, Snark whirled around and made a grab for the gun. Burnett stepped out of range. Snark lost his balance and fell to one knee. He lunged forward and attempted to grasp Burnett's ankle, and Burnett struck him on the head with the barrel of the pistol. Snark lost all interest in trying to escape and fell forward on his face.

Burnett waited for the sheriff to regain consciousness and then toed him in the ribs.

'Try that again and you won't see the inside of the jail,' Burnett said. 'Get up and let's move on.'

They reached the jail without further incident. Snark tried the door. It was locked. He rattled the handle and a voice within called out a challenge.

'It's Snark. Open the door.'

Burnett jabbed Snark in the back with his pistol when the door opened. The jailer, Seth Johnson, stepped back out of the entrance, surprised by the sight of the gun in Burnett's hand.

'What's going on?' Johnson demanded.

'Snark is under arrest,' Burnett said. 'He was involved in robbing the bank about six months ago.'

'That's a lie,' Snark said. 'Someone's spreading lies, trying to get even with me.'

'I don't have time to go into it now,'

Burnett told him. 'It's a charge that will hold you until I can get around to making inquiries. Lock him in a cell, Johnson. Empty his pockets first, and don't give him any chance to get the better of you. He's not to see or talk to anyone until I say so. Got that?'

'Whatever you say.' Johnson picked up his keys.

Burnett followed Johnson, who ushered Snark into the cells, and watched his incarceration. Snark sat down on the bunk inside the cell and folded his arms. He did not show any emotion, but smiled as Burnett turned away.

'It seems strange, having the sheriff locked in his own cells,' said Johnson.

'You'd better get used to it,' Burnett told him. 'And there'll be others in here before too long. Has there been any trouble in town since this afternoon?'

'Nothing I've heard about. Are you expecting trouble, Marshal?'

'I hope there won't be any. I'm gonna take a look around. Be ready for anything, huh?'

Johnson nodded, and Burnett departed. He went back to the diner, and the waitress intercepted him at the door of the kitchen.

'Your friend left by the back door when you took the sheriff out to the street,' she said.

'Aw, hell!' Burnett heaved a sigh of exasperation. 'Did he say where he was going?'

'Not a word. But he was in a hurry when he left.'

'Did you see which way he went?'

'No. It's dark outside.'

Burnett considered for a moment, and then departed. He hoped Lance had gone to see Susan Blaine, and hurried along the street to check. He was disappointed to find the Blaine house in total darkness, and resisted the impulse to disturb the girl. He stood for some minutes in the shadows, but there were no sounds or movement in the street.

He was not pleased that Lance had left. He needed to have a long talk with his brother to clear up a number of the incidents that had occurred in the past, and he suspected that Lance had broken the law while he was being ousted from B7 by Grint's crew. He just hoped that Lance was not implicated in the bank robbery.

There was little he could do now, and so he returned to the law office. He had Snark brought out of the cell into the front office, and Johnson stood behind the sheriff while Burnett fired questions at the prisoner. But the sheriff remained silent, shaking his head at each question, and Burnett realized that he was wasting his time.

'You won't get away with anything by refusing to answer questions,' Burnett said at length. He motioned to Johnson. 'Put him back in his cell. I'll talk to him again later.'

Snark went back to his cell and Johnson returned.

'I've been thinking about the raid on Blaine's bank,' Johnson said. 'There was a lot of talk about it at the time, and your brother's name was mentioned more than once. I don't know who started that talk, but it caught on and folks began to think Lance Burnett did the robbery.'

'I'll get to the bottom of it before I'm through,' Burnett said. 'I listen to rumours, but I work on facts, and they are what I accept.'

He wondered where Lance was at that moment, and restlessness filled him as he considered his brother's part in the wider scheme of things. So far he had only heard one side of Lance's activities. He decided to talk to Susan Blaine again first thing in the morning.

'I'd better make Snark's round of the town, seeing that he's unable to do it,' he told Johnson.

'Do you think that's a good idea?' the jailer asked. 'I've heard talk that Brent Weedon is out to get you, and this time of the day is when he's likely to drop on to you.'

'The day I fear bad men is the day I'll hand in my law badge,' Burnett said sharply. 'You take care of your side of the business and I'll attend to mine.'

Johnson shrugged as Burnett went to the street door.

'It's your funeral,' he observed.

Burnett went out to the silent street and stood in the shadows to check his surroundings. His thoughts were remote now, pushed into the back of his mind by the eternal pressure of duty. There was only one shaft of yellow light visible along the street and that came from the big saloon. He pictured Mack Brown, jealous of his wife and a rustler who had been caught in the act. Was there any truth in Brown's statement that he had given Lance two hundred dollars to finance his getaway six months ago? If he had, then it suggested that there had been a very close relationship between them, for Burnett sensed that Brown was not a man to throw his money around.

He stopped the flow of his thoughts and went towards the saloon, making no sound in his approach and staying in the thickest shadows. He moved from doorway to doorway, pausing to check and recheck his surroundings, his hand on the butt of his gun, his reflexes strained for instant reaction to any unnatural sound.

When he reached the front of the saloon he was surprised to see two horses standing at the hitch rail, and he remained motionless for some minutes, listening and watching. The door to the entrance of the saloon was closed behind the batwings. He leaned sideways and looked through a window. The big room of the saloon was in darkness. The light inside was coming through a half open door that gave access to Brown's office.

Burnett tried the door of the saloon and found it locked. So who had come into town very late and entered Brown's domain? Burnett eased into the alley beside the saloon and made his way to the back lot, feeling his way through the darkness. He could have cut his initials on the dense blackness, and with his eyes useless in the night, he had to rely on his ears to check his surroundings.

When he reached the rear corner of the saloon he saw lamp light streaming out of Brown's office window, and his instincts warned him to stay away from it. But he needed a breakthrough in this situation and steeled himself to make the effort to spotlight himself although he was aware that any of his enemies could be waiting in the surrounding shadows to kill him.

He went forward, gun in hand now, and stepped up to the window, his teeth clenched in anticipation of a shot in the back. He peered into the lighted office, saw Brown seated at his desk, faced by Rafe Callow and another gunman from Grint's ranch; his brother Lance was seated on a chair beside the desk, leaning back at ease and smoking a cigar.

Burnett was shocked, but his wits were not affected. He dropped to all fours, crawled away from the window and, as he got to his feet beyond the shaft of lamp light, a gun flash shredded the night and threw a string of echoes across the silent town. The bullet thudded into the wall beside the window. Burnett ran swiftly for the cover of an alley and ducked into it. He stood just inside, gun ready, but the echoes faded and growled away and nothing more happened.

As he turned and faded into the night he heard the sound of the back door of the saloon being jerked open and men's voices raised in shock and surprise. He paused to watch Brown and Callow emerge through the back door and stand looking around into the shadows, guns out and ready for action. Lance emerged a moment later and hurried away into the night before Burnett could think of stopping him. He dared not give chase while Brown and Callow were outside, and when they eventually went back into the saloon it was too late to chase after Lance.

He went to the back door as a bolt was pushed home on the inside, sensing it was time for action, and rapped on the door with the butt of his pistol. He cocked the weapon as the door was unbolted again, and levelled it as the door was dragged open . . .

9

Mack Brown jerked the saloon door open. He was still holding his gun, but apparently expected someone he knew to be waiting. Burnett thrust his pistol up until the muzzle was almost touching Brown's nose. Brown uttered an imprecation, but froze.

'Drop your gun,' Burnett snapped.

Brown opened his fingers and the gun thudded on the floor. Callow pushed forward, saw Burnett, and spun away to run. Burnett thrust Brown aside and aimed at Callow's leg. The crash of the shot rocked the saloon and echoes blasted. Callow fell instantly, hit in the back of his right thigh just above the knee. Brown dropped to his hands and knees and tried to scoop up his pistol. Burnett struck the back of his head and Brown fell flat on his face.

Callow was shouting in pain, clasping his leg with both hands. Blood was seeping through the cloth of his pants. The man accompanying Callow stuck his head out of the office. He began to withdraw, and Burnett called to him.

'Stand still. Get your hands up and come out of the office.'

For a moment the man remained motionless, staring at Callow, and then he raised his hands and stepped out of the office. Burnett went forward and disarmed him before picking up Callow's gun. He went back to Brown, who was unconscious, and kicked Brown's discarded gun into the nearest corner. Then he turned to his unwounded prisoner.

'Have you got a name?' he demanded.

'Joe Marlow.'

Callow looked up at Burnett, his face twisted in agony. 'For Chris'sakes get me to the doctor before I bleed to death,' he rasped. 'What did you have to shoot me for?'

'You shouldn't have tried to run,'

Burnett said. 'You're facing a charge of kidnapping, and I'm the witness, seeing it was me you removed from Grint's house.'

'Where is Snark?' Callow demanded. 'I wanta talk to him.'

'I'll put you in his cell and you can talk then. What was your business with Brown?'

'I've got nothing to say.'

Burnett nodded. 'It's OK by me if you want to do it the hard way.'

When Brown regained his senses, Burnett compelled him and Marlow to carry Callow to the law office. The trio were then locked in cells. Burnett left in a hurry, but knocked up the doctor and told him to check on Callow. He hurried along the street, went to the Blaine house, and knocked on the door when he saw a light inside a downstairs room. Susan came to the door. She was in a dressing gown and her hair was untidy.

'I need to talk to Lance,' Burnett said.

'What makes you think he's here?' she countered.

'Don't play games with me,' he snapped. 'I know he's here. The house was in complete darkness when I checked some time ago. Lance is here, and I want to see him. It's for his good health, so if you care about him then show me in.'

Susan sighed and opened the door wide. Burnett entered and walked into the lighted room. Lance was seated on a couch, and sprang to his feet when he saw his brother.

'Sit down,' Burnett said roughly, and Lance dropped back into his seat. 'What were you doing in Mack Brown's office?

'So it was you prowling around outside, huh? What's with Brown? Have you got something against him? He was a good friend to me six months ago, when I was up against it. Why shouldn't I visit him?'

'I told you to wait at the diner for me. I don't need to have to keep an eye on you when I've got a job to do. I'm trying to clean up around here, and you ain't helping.'

'I'm sorry about that. I've also got things to do. There are men around here I need to settle with. Some of them gave me a bad time when Grint was forcing me out.'

'I reckon to pick up Grint and his outfit as soon as I can,' Burnett snapped.

'If you talk to me nicely I might pitch in and give you a hand.' Lance grinned.

Burnett heaved a sigh. 'If you levelled with me my job might pan out easier. I get the impression you're hiding something from me, Lance.'

'Why should you think I've done something wrong? I'm the one who's been wronged. I had a lot of trouble just because I was running B7 for you. Anybody else would have cut and run as soon as Grint started throwing his weight around. But the ranch belonged to you, and I've always believed that blood is thicker than water. I stuck at it and took the trouble because you are my brother. I could have done with you being around when I was up against it, but I had to face it alone and, now it's payback time, you're here and getting in my way.'

'I'm concerned about you.' Burnett shook his head. 'I'm sorry for the way the cards fell when I wasn't around. That's why I'm trying to make it easy for you now. Who robbed the bank six months ago?'

Lance glanced at Susan, who was standing by the door listening to their conversation. She moved restlessly when their attention turned to her, and then heaved a sigh.

'I'd like to know the answer to that question too,' she said. 'Who did rob the bank? Do you know, Lance?'

'Hey, you don't think it was me, do you?' He shook his head. 'As far as I know, it was Snark and Hoyle did the robbery, and I hate to say this, Susan, but your father arranged it. He got those poor excuses for lawmen to rob his bank. But it didn't go as planned. They were supposed to hand the money over to your father afterwards, but it went missing and he didn't get it.'

'What happened to it?' Burnett demanded.

'Why ask me?' Lance shrugged. 'I don't know. Ask the men who stole it.'

Burnett moved restlessly. 'I'll do that. You'll be staying here now, I guess. Just be here in the morning when I call to talk to you.'

'Sure thing.' Lance smiled.

Burnett departed. He was not happy with the situation. He suspected that Lance was playing some deep game of his own, but he was not a speculative man, and fixed his mind on the broader aspects of the case. He needed to pick up Grint and his outfit, locate Hoyle and arrest him, and discover the whereabouts of the stolen bank money. Everything else would fall into line if he accomplished those things, and anything else would be purely incidental — like Weedon, the gun man.

He returned to the law office. Johnson opened the door to him, bleary-eyed and yawning.

'Everything is quiet in here, Marshal,' he reported.

'I need to talk to Snark now,' Burnett said.

'He's snoring like a pig in his cell. It'll give me a lot of pleasure to wake him.' Johnson grinned and went into the cell block. Moments later he ushered Snark into the office. Snark rubbed his eyes and glowered at Burnett.

'This is the helluva time to drag a man out of his cell,' he grated.

'It won't take a moment. Tell me who robbed the bank six months ago, and what happened to the money.'

'If I knew where the money is I wouldn't still be hanging around here. I'd have picked it up and shook the dust of this place off my boots. It was hidden away, and when we went for it someone had taken it.'

'Who was with you on the robbery?'

'You know Hoyle was with me. There was no one else.'

'Are you sure there was no one else?'

'We didn't need anyone else. Blaine arranged for us to walk in and take the dough. He expected us to hand it back to him afterwards, the poor sap! He expected us to be satisfied with a handful of dollars! Instead, we went for all of it.'

'Naturally. Blaine was a fool if he really thought you would return it. Where did you hide the money?'

'It was buried out of town.'

'Where?'

Snark grinned mirthlessly. 'This'll kill you! We hid it in the storm cellar out at B7. Your place had been burned out, and no one ever went out there, so we got the idea that it would be safe in that cellar. But there was someone always prowling around that place.' Snark lifted his gaze and looked into Burnett's eyes. 'Your brother Lance!'

'Are you saying Lance stole the money from you?'

Snark shook his head. 'We couldn't ever catch him to ask him. But it looked like he took it.'

Burnett blinked his tired eyes. He felt ready to drop, and knew it was time that he got some sleep.

'OK, put him back in his cell, Johnson. I'm going off duty now, but I'll be back first thing in the morning.'

'You look like you can do with some shut-eye,' Johnson observed.

Burnett waited until Johnson returned from locking Snark in his cell and then departed for the hotel. When he reached his room he merely removed his gun-belt and dropped wearily on the bed; he was asleep almost immediately. It seemed that only a few minutes had passed when the sun shone through the window and disturbed him.

He was not fully revived from the toils of the day before, but he was accustomed to long hours, discomfort, and dangerous work. He buckled on his gun-belt, and took the time to clean and oil his pistol and check his supply of .45 shells. He was hungry, but went first to the law office, where Johnson was rousing the prisoners in their cells. As soon as Burnett showed his face Mack Brown, standing at the bars of his cell door, called out. Burnett went to him.

'How long are you gonna keep me in here?' Brown rasped. 'I've got a business to run.'

'You should have thought of that before you started mixing with the bad guys around here. I've got some inquiries to make about you, Brown. You were caught rustling Grint's cows once, and I expect charges will result from that.'

'Rustling cattle?' Brown cursed. 'Hell, I'm a saloon man. The nearest I've been to a steer is a beef steak on my plate. Who told you I've rustled cattle? Bring him here and let him accuse me to my face.'

'You'll get your chance, but not today. I've got something to do now that will probably take all day. I'll get around to you later, Brown.'

Snark was seated on his bunk, arms folded; his face was expressionless. Burnett confronted him.

'Have you got anything to add to what you told me last night?' Burnett demanded.

'The hell I have!' Snark replied.

Burnett turned to the watchful Johnson. 'You'll have to arrange breakfast for your guests, Johnson, and you'll need help. What time do you go off duty?'

'Eight o'clock this morning but I'll help with the breakfast before I leave.'

'I want a posse to take out to Big G. It's time I pulled in Grint and his outfit.'

'You'll need to see Lew Chaston, the town mayor. He runs the Mercantile along the street. He'll see you right.'

'I'll have some breakfast and then call on him. Do you have any problems?'

'No, everything is OK. The place will be overcrowded if you bring in all Grint's outfit.'

'I'll bring them in if they've broken the law,' Burnett said.

After having breakfast, Burnett walked into the large store. A tall, lean man in his early thirties was serving a woman at the big counter, and he lifted a hand to Burnett.

'Be with you shortly. I won't be a minute.'

'Take your time,' Burnett replied. He remained in the background, looking around the store, taking in the various smells of the provisions and leather goods.

Lew Chaston came out from behind the counter. His blue eyes had a piercing quality, and he gazed at Burnett with something akin to admiration showing plainly in his eyes.

'How can I help you, Marshal?' he asked.

'I need a posse to ride out with me. There will probably be action, and I hope to arrest several men.'

'That will be no problem. How many men do you reckon you'll need?'

'About ten or twelve, and I want to be riding as soon as possible.'

'I'll get my wife to take over in here and then round up some regular posse men for you. Shall I tell them to meet you at the livery barn?'

'That would be good. I'll be ready to ride from the stable in thirty minutes.'

'I'll ride with you,' Chaston said. 'How are you off for shells?'

'Thanks for the reminder. I'll take a box of .45s and a box of 44.40s. And there's a point I ought to raise now. Sheriff Snark is under arrest. I've got several prisoners in the cells and only the night jailer guarding them at the moment. Can you put a reliable man in the office to handle matters? He'll need to wear a law badge and have some authority.'

'I know just the man. I'll have a word with him.'

Burnett left the store with his ammunition and walked to the Blaine house. Susan answered his knock, and one look at her taut face caused

Burnett's heart to turn over.

'Where's Lance?' he demanded.

'He left before sunup,' she replied. 'I tried to get him to stay but he said he had some unfinished business to handle and told me to tell you he'll see you later.'

'I should have locked him in a cell last night,' Burnett said. 'Why can't he ever do what he's told?'

'He had a lot of trouble six months ago, and remained true to you. He almost died trying to save B7 so don't be too hard on him. He's a good man. I trust him.'

'I wish I could.' Burnett shook his head. 'Did he give you any idea what he's planning to do?'

'You know he always plays his cards close to his vest. Whatever he's got in mind to do, the outcome will be in your best interests.'

'I hope you're right. If he does come back then tell him to stay here until I show again.'

He departed, aware that time was

fleeting, and dropped by Doc Willard's office. The doctor was out on a call but his wife was there, and Burnett asked after Henry Blaine.

'He's still not out of the woods yet,' Mrs Willard said, 'but we think he'll pull through.'

The news cheered Burnett somewhat, for Susan's sake. He went back to the law office and found that breakfast was being served to the prisoners. Johnson was being assisted by another jailer, and Burnett was satisfied that everything was under control.

'Johnson, I'm taking out a posse now,' he told the jailer. 'It's Grint's turn to be brought in.'

'I wish you luck,' Johnson replied. 'We'll be here when you get back.'

Burnett went along to the livery barn. Posse men were beginning to gather there, saddling up and checking weapons. A big man, who seemed to be in charge of the proceedings, came to Burnett's side. He was well-muscled; his blue eyes were clear and bright in a clean-cut, finely chiselled face. His shirt sleeves were rolled up tightly on his brawny arms.

'Marshal, I'm Mike Arkwright, and I usually handle the posse,' he said. 'There'll be about a dozen men all told. The word has gone around town. Can you tell me where we'll be heading? It looks like being a big job.'

'We're going to Grint's Big G ranch. I want Grint under arrest, and any of his outfit who might resist. We shall be looking for Rufus Hoyle. He's wounded, and won't want to come in, but he's wanted for suspected bank robbery, among other things. That's about it.'

'It's about time something was done about the trouble we're getting hereabouts. Snark ain't no great shakes as a lawman. He let a lot of things slide.'

'He's no longer the sheriff. I put him in the cells last night; charges pending. Let's get ready to ride, huh?'

The posse assembled outside the barn — ordinary townsmen who were ready to risk life and limb for the law. Arkwright waited for a couple of stragglers to arrive, and then the posse rode out, Burnett leading with Arkwright at his side. They rode at a steady, mile-eating lope, heading for Big G, and Burnett felt the doubts and fears in his mind beginning to fade into the background as they continued. The law was on the march, honest men moving to confront the lawless, and there was no doubt in Burnett's mind as to the outcome of their foray.

10

When he sighted Big G, Burnett called a halt and the posse men gathered around him. He looked at unsmiling, tense faces. Most of the men drew their weapons, checked them, and returned them to their holsters. There was an air of grim determination among the score of temporary lawmen, and Burnett knew he would be well served by them.

'We're here to arrest Grint and any of his men who show resistance to our purpose,' Burnett said. 'Arkwright, perhaps you'll take five men; circle to the rear of the ranch and work your way forward. I'll go in by the front yard and call on Grint to surrender. We'll play it as it comes. If they don't surrender then we'll have to do it the hard way. Watch out for Rufus Hoyle. He's wounded, and hiding out here.

Take him prisoner if you can. That's all. Let's get on with it.'

Arkwright led five posse men away on a detour. Burnett waited to give them time to get into position and then led the remainder of the posse into the yard of the ranch. They spread out as they approached the house, and Burnett signalled for them to halt some yards out from the porch. He continued alone to rein up facing the front door of the house.

As he halted, Burnett glanced at his surroundings, noting that the ranch was silent and still, with no sign of life anywhere. There was no work being done around the yard, and only a few horses were in the corral. The bunkhouse looked derelict. When he called, his voice echoed eerily across the yard.

'Amos Grint, this is Burnett, a deputy US marshal, heading a lawful posse from Pike's Crossing. Come out unarmed.'

There was no reply, and Burnett stepped down from his saddle as the sound of his voice died away. He motioned for the posse men to remain where they were and stepped on to the porch, his right hand resting on the butt of his holstered gun. He reached out with his left hand and tried the door, which swung open at his touch, and he stepped inside, pausing on the threshold to announce his presence.

'Is there anyone in the house?' he called.

There was no reply, but suddenly he heard footsteps out back, and swung to face the door of the kitchen as it was pushed open. An old man wearing a white apron came into view. He halted in surprise.

'Who in hell are you?' he demanded.

'Where's Amos Grint?'

'The boss ain't here. He rode out at sunup with the whole outfit — said something about sorting out some trouble that's come up. He reckoned he'd be back by noon. Now tell me who you are.'

'Marshal Burnett. I've got a posse

outside in the yard. What's your name?'

'I'm Will Gartree. I've been the cook on this spread twenty years.'

'OK, Gartree, so where's Grint gone?'

'I don't rightly know, seeing that he never told me. And I've learned over the years never to ask questions that don't concern me.'

'What direction did he take when he left?'

'I got no idea, seeing it was still dark when he rode outa the yard. If you wanta see him then you'll have to wait for his return. I'll get back to my cooking. The boss will wanta eat when he rides in.'

'Stand where you are. Grint won't be eating here again. His next meal will be behind bars in the local jail. I'm arresting you for questioning, Gartree.'

'I ain't done nothing wrong, and I sure as hell don't know anything. Let me get back to my cooking.'

Burnett went out to the porch and waved to the posse to close in. They dismounted at the porch, turning outwards to watch the approaches to the ranch while Burnett explained the situation. Hoofs sounded at the side of the house, and then Arkwright and the five men with him appeared. They reined in and dismounted.

'I saw a rider on that ridge over there,' said Arkwright, pointing to the right. 'He rode back over the crest when he saw us.'

'There's a bunch of riders coming in on the back trail,' someone warned.

Burnett turned and spotted movement beyond the ranch. A dozen riders were travelling at a canter on a trail coming from the north.

'It's Grint in the lead,' Arkwright said instantly. 'I reckon we should take up positions to receive them, Marshal.'

'Fan out around the yard and cover them,' Burnett said without hesitation. 'No shooting, unless they start it.'

The posse men went at a run across the yard, spreading out and finding what cover they could. Burnett remained on the porch with Arkwright at his side. Amos Grint pounded into the yard and angled for the porch, his outfit following closely. He reined up in a cloud of dust and stepped down from his saddle, hand on the butt of his holstered gun. He gazed at Burnett as if they were strangers.

'What are you doing on my porch?' Grint demanded.

'Waiting for you,' Burnett replied. 'Where have you been?'

'I don't have to answer your questions,' Grint snarled. 'Who are you to come in here throwing your weight about?'

Burnett was aware that the riders who were backing Grint were still mounted, and most of them had their hands on their gun butts.

'I was here yesterday,' Burnett said. 'Callow brought me in as a prisoner. So I'm back now to arrest you for harbouring a wanted criminal — Rufus Hoyle — and for consorting with known criminals.'

'You're gonna arrest me?' Grint laughed. 'You sure got ambitions, mister.'

'Raise your hands and come quietly,' Burnett rapped. 'A posse is surrounding you, and ready for action.'

Grint looked around, shaking his head. 'Nobody comes in here and orders me around,' he said. 'Hamblin, you're bossing my gun crew now, so do something about the posse.'

'What do you suggest, boss?' one of riders demanded. 'The posse men have got us covered all ways to the middle.'

Burnett glanced at the speaker out of a corner of his eye; he saw a big man wearing two guns on crossed cartridge belts sitting his horse within the grouped outfit. The man's face was beaded with sweat and covered in dust. He looked over-heated, and his expression was evincing doubt.

'What the hell do I pay you for?' Grint demanded. 'Pull your guns and get them fellers out of my yard.'

'You want them out then do it

yourself,' Hamblin replied. 'I ain't tangling with the law. They're loaded for bear. The one wearing the law badge is a deputy US marshal, and I learned years ago that you don't tangle with his kind.'

Grint cursed and reached for his gun, drawing fast, but Burnett, watching him intently, was activated by the rancher's initial move. His gun appeared in his hand and blasted raucously before Grint could fire. The bullet smacked into Grint's right shoulder and he fell backwards on the porch, his gun dropping to the dusty boards.

Burnett turned to face the riders. None of them had moved to back Grint. They gazed impassively at Burnett.

'Grint is under arrest,' Burnett said. 'Anyone trying to side with him will be breaking the law and I'll be obliged to make more arrests. You riders head across to the corral, unsaddle your mounts, and then stay in the bunkhouse until I can get around to talking to you.

If Rufus Hoyle is on the ranch, bring him out here to me.'

The outfit moved away across the yard. Arkwright heaved a sigh before going to Grint's side.

'That panned out well,' Arkwright said, 'but I think we should disarm those men. They could change their minds any time.'

'Not while we've got Grint,' Burnett replied. 'Take him into the house and guard him. Fix his shoulder, if you can. We'll be heading back to town shortly. Have some of the men search the spread for Hoyle. He was here yesterday, and he's carrying a bullet hole. I need him behind bars. I'll talk to Grint before we ride back to town. I need to know where he went this morning.'

'Raising hell with his neighbours, no doubt,' Arkwright said. He called to a posse man standing nearby. 'Give me a hand, Billy. We'll patch up Grint and get him ready to ride into town.'

Burnett went across to the bunkhouse. The riders who had accompanied Grint had left their mounts saddled in the corral and were already there. Burnett motioned three of the posse men to accompany him and entered himself. He confronted Hamblin, the gun man.

'So where did you ride with Grint this morning?' Burnett demanded.

'Did Grint tell you where we went?'

'He's in no fit state to talk at the moment.'

'Then you'll have to wait until he can tell you.' Hamblin spoke smoothly. 'I don't want any trouble with the law, Marshal, but Grint is the boss and he'll do the talking when the time comes.'

'Is Rufus Hoyle on the spread?'

Hamblin shook his head. 'I saw him around yesterday but not today. Maybe he pulled out when we wasn't looking.'

Burnett realized that he would get no co-operation from these hard cases. He looked around at intent faces, saw animosity in cold eyes, and dropped his hand to the butt of his gun.

'I can arrest you for refusing to help the law,' he said harshly, 'and I'm in no mood to play games. Tell me what I wanta know or you'll all see the inside of the jail. So I'll ask the question again. Where did you ride this morning with Grint?'

'Let me ask a question before you get down to cases,' Hamblin said. 'What's going to happen to Grint now you've arrested him?'

'He'll be investigated, and will stand trial on any charges that arise. Right now I've got him for resisting arrest and harbouring a wanted man, and I don't doubt there will be other charges when we probe his association with Sheriff Snark, who is now under arrest.'

'So he'll spend time in prison, huh?' said Hamblin.

'You can bet on it,' Burnett replied.

'Then the way I see it, we're wasting our time sticking around here, so I quit, and I'm getting out right now.' Hamblin looked into Burnett's eyes. 'Is that OK with you?'

'Sure. The only option for you is jail, so make up your mind, and if you've got any sense you'll hit the trail.'

Hamblin turned and left the bunkhouse, followed by the rest of the outfit. Burnett heaved an inaudible sigh of relief. He stood for a moment, considering the situation, and started in shock when gunshots broke the silence and heavy echoes drifted across the ranch. He ran out of the bunkhouse to the corral.

Hamblin and rest of the outfit were in the corral, guns drawn. Two of them were facedown, unmoving in the dust. Burnett looked around, wondering if the posse had fired the shots. He saw Arkwright running towards him from the ranch house. The blacksmith was pointing away to the left, and when he reached Burnett he paused to catch his breath.

'I saw gunsmoke coming from a knoll about fifty yards beyond the corral,' he gasped. 'There was one man, and he rode out fast after shooting.'

'Keep control of the situation here,' Burnett said sharply. 'I'll ride out and look for the ambusher. It could be someone who had a call from Grint and his outfit this morning.'

Burnett ran to the porch and untied his horse. He set off at a gallop for the spot from which the ambusher had fired, and slithered out of the saddle when he reached the knoll. He didn't expect to find the ambusher, and looked around for signs that someone had used the spot to shoot down two of Grint's outfit. He found two empty 44.40 shells glinting in the long grass, picked them up, and dropped them into his pocket.

When he straightened to check his surroundings he caught sight of a rider sitting his horse on a nearby ridge, and reached into a saddle-bag for his long range glasses. He focused on the man, and was shocked when he was able to make out details: it was his brother Lance. Burnett saw blood on the left sleeve of Lance's shirt. Lance raised his right hand and waved, obviously recognizing him, and then turned his horse and rode off the skyline.

Burnett heaved a sigh, stifling the impulse to chase after Lance. He had his duty to do, and his brother would have to wait. He watched the ridge for some minutes but Lance did not reappear. Burnett turned away and went back to the ranch, his thoughts churning.

'There's no one out there now,' he told Arkwright. He saw Grint's outfit riding out of the ranch, leaving their dead in the corral.

'We're ready to head back to town,' Arkwright replied. 'Grint is able to travel.'

'Who are the two dead men in the corral?' Burnett asked.

'A couple of hard cases named Jennings and Krantz. The ambusher shot them without warning.'

'I'll check it out later,' Burnett said. 'Let's get outa here.'

The trip back to town was uneventful, and a sense of anti-climax gripped the posse men when they sighted the town. Arkwright looked at Burnett.

'Shall we disband the posse now?' he demanded.

'I guess so. I reckon I can handle matters around town. Thanks for your help. I'll take Grint in from here.'

He took the lead rope on Grint's horse from one of the posse men and continued along the street. The posse men turned into the stable. Burnett drooped in his saddle but stiffened his shoulders. He was worried about his brother. Lance had been in action earlier and had apparently tangled with Grint's outfit. Two of Grint's men had been murdered, and Lance would have to answer for the shooting.

Burnett stopped off at the doctor's house and left Grint with Doc Willard.

'You can talk to Blaine now, if you wish,' said the doctor. 'He's been asking to see you. He's in the back room along the hall.'

'Thanks, Doc. I need to have a word with him.'

Burnett went to the room that Doctor Willard used as a hospital.

There were three beds in it, all occupied, and Blaine was propped up in the one nearest the door. The banker was pale-faced. He was swathed in bandages around his upper body. His eyes were open and he nodded when he saw Burnett.

'I've had time to think since you shot me,' he said in a low tone. 'I guess I asked for what's happened, but I was desperate. Now I'm sorry, and it's too late. But I want to tell you about the man who made my trouble worse. He horned into the deal unasked — through Hoyle — and called all the shots after the robbery. He wanted your brother framed for stealing the money, and he hounded Lance until he disappeared.'

'What's his name?' Burnett demanded.

'Brent Weedon, Grint's top gun.'

'I'll pick him up,' Burnett said. 'Is there anything else?'

Blaine closed his eyes. Burnett studied his face for a moment before departing quietly.

He went to the law office, found it locked, and looked through the front window. There was no one inside. He frowned. A voice hailed him from along the street and he turned to see the jailer, Seth Johnson, coming towards him. Relief filled Burnett. He had begun to think that trouble in town had erupted while he was away. But Johnson was smiling. He came up and unlocked the office door.

'I had to slip out,' Johnson explained. 'I need some extra hands around here, and I've arranged for a couple of men to come in and help out. We've got too many prisoners for two men to cope with safely. One or two of the prisoners are getting fractious — Snark in particular. He's been threatening me, hinting that something bad could happen to my family if I don't turn him loose. But don't worry. I'm used to that kinda talk from prisoners.'

'I'll be around now,' Burnett said, 'and I'll be on hand to help. I arrested Grint out at his ranch, and he stopped a slug in his shoulder before he agreed to come quietly. He's at the doc's place now. I'll check on him later, and bring him over if he's fit to move after Doc has finished with him.'

Burnett entered the office and went through to the cells. He looked over his prisoners, and realized that he had to deal with a pile of legal procedure and endless interrogations before he could put any one of them in front of a judge. He confronted Snark, who was seated on his bunk, gazing at the floor in silent contemplation of his situation.

'Have you got any complaints, Snark?' Burnett demanded.

The ex-sheriff looked up at him, shook his head, and then ignored him. Burnett went back into the office.

'I need to have a meal, and then I'll take a look around town,' he told Johnson. 'There are one or two things I have to check on. But I won't be far away. You're doing a great job, Johnson. We'll soon get the town back to normal.'

'I can hold my own,' the jailer replied. 'You do what you have to.'

Burnett departed and went to the diner for a meal. He was aware of tension in the back of his mind, and realized that he was subconsciously looking for Brent Weedon to appear. The gunman had said he wanted a shootout, and Burnett guessed that he would show when least expected. He considered the situation while waiting for his meal, and reckoned that he had arrested everyone who figured in the investigation except Rufus Hoyle. There were still several points that needed to be clarified, but it was obvious now that his brother Lance had most of the answers.

He ate his meal quickly and then walked along the darkened street, hoping the cool night breeze would clear his riotous thoughts. He was tired and wanted to call it a day, but his mind was too active, and he knew he would not sleep if he tried. He walked along Main Street, intending to return to the jail and begin interrogating his prisoners. Just then, a female voice called his name, and he turned to see Abbie Brown emerging from the front door of the darkened saloon.

'Hi, Abbie,' he greeted. 'I've been meaning to drop in and see you, but I've been real busy today.'

'I know,' she replied. 'You've been arresting men all over town, including my husband. Are you charging him with anything?'

'I don't know yet. But you sound like you wouldn't be surprised if I did.'

'Mack is not a nice man to know. I wouldn't be surprised if you kept him locked up and threw away the key. But your brother Lance is bothering me. He's in the saloon, and I want you to get him out. He says he's waiting for someone to turn up, and he's in Mack's office. I've told him the saloon isn't open for business, but he won't leave.'

'Lance is in the saloon?' Burnett's voice was harsh. 'Heck, I've been trying to track him down. Who's he waiting to see, did he say?'

Abbie shook her head. She was uneasy. Burnett noted her manner and started towards the saloon.

'Let's confront him and see what he has to say.'

They walked to the batwings of the saloon, and Abbie paused when Burnett pushed open the swing doors. The interior of the saloon was unlit and shadowed. Dim light was shining through the half-opened door of the office at the rear of the big barroom.

'I won't come in,' Abbie said. 'I don't know what Lance has been up to, but his left arm is soaked in dried blood, and he's talking wild. Please get him out of here, Cal, and don't let him come back, especially now Mack is in jail.'

'Come inside and sit at one of the tables until I've taken Lance out,' Burnett suggested.

She did so, and remained motionless as he crossed the saloon heading for the office in the passage leading to the back door. As he entered the passage he could hear the sound of voices in the office. He moved closer to the half-open office door and paused to listen.

'What in hell do you want, Hoyle?' Lance was saying, and at the mention of Hoyle's name Burnett drew his pistol and cocked it.

'What do you think I want?' Hoyle replied. 'I want that dough Blaine gave Snark and me in the bank.'

'How many times do I have to tell you that I don't know anything about that dough?'

'You were hiding out in the storm cellar in the ruins of B7 six months ago, and that's where I hid it. No one else has been around there, and when I went back for it, it was gone. It's got to be you who took it, and I want it back, see.'

'You put a slug in me six months ago, and I damn near died. I left town and stayed away for months. I never saw the bank dough. You'll have to look elsewhere for who took it. All I can tell you is that when I came back a month ago I saw some of Grint's outfit showing a lot of interest in the ruins on B7. Weedon and Sawtell hardly let a day go by without looking around there. At the time I wondered what they were after, and now I guess it must have been the bank dough.'

'I don't believe you, and I'm getting mighty short of patience. I need that dough now Snark is behind bars. Is it in that safe in the corner there? You got almighty friendly with Mack Brown all of a sudden.'

'The best thing you can do, Hoyle, is see the doctor. You look like you're dying on your feet.'

'I'm OK. And I ain't going anywhere without that money.' Hoyle spoke doggedly. 'What are you doing in here, anyway? Mack Brown is in jail.'

'I'm waiting for someone.'

'Another crooked deal, huh?'

'You're one to talk. Who's been doing all the bad stuff around here? I'll bet it was you and Snark. You robbed the bank for Blaine, and kept the dough. There were two other bank jobs in the county that I know for a certainty were done by you and Snark. And I heard today that the stage coach was held up and robbed and the shotgun guard was killed. You again, I reckon.'

Hoyle cursed, and Burnett, hearing the rasp of a pistol being drawn, kicked open the half-open door and lunged forward, gun lifting. He saw Lance seated at the desk. Hoyle was standing before the desk, his gun lifting to cover Lance. Burnett kept moving, reached Hoyle's side, and slammed his gun barrel against Hoyle's gun hand as the crooked deputy levelled his Colt at Lance.

Hoyle's gun blasted, but Burnett's blow caused the weapon to jerk off target. The bullet struck the metal safe in a corner as the crash of the shot filled the room. Hoyle dropped his gun and grasped his right hand. He was unsteady on his feet. His shirt was drenched with blood from the wound Burnett had given him earlier. His face was pale, and he staggered. Burnett struck his left temple with a back-handed blow with his pistol and Hoyle fell to the floor and remained motion-less.

Lance sprang to his feet, his face showing shock. He stared at Hoyle, and then looked at Burnett.

'Where in hell did you come from?' he gasped, dropping his hand to his gun butt.

'I've been looking for you ever since I saw you out at Grint's place earlier, Lance. You murdered two of Grint's outfit. You saw me, and waved before you made tracks. You shot those two men from cover out at Grint's place. Is that why you ran?'

'I didn't shoot them,' Lance said. 'I got there just as the shots were fired, and I saw the man who fired them — Brent Weedon. He took off fast, and when you came out from the ranch I didn't stay around. I told you I'd come

248

and talk to you when I was good and ready.' Lance grimaced. 'I had to bring Hoyle out in the open, and now there's someone else I need to see before this is done, and I'm expecting him to show up here any time. You better get out before he comes or I won't get the chance to nail him.'

'I can't do that.' Burnett pointed his gun at Lance. 'I'm gonna jail you for murder. I can't take your word that Weedon did the shooting. Get your hand off your gun, Lance. I'm arresting you.'

Lance was standing beside the desk. Burnett had his back to the office door, and Hoyle, gasping for breath, was lying at his feet. Burnett saw Lance's face change expression and, when Lance suddenly drew his gun, Burnett responded instinctively. He cocked his gun and, when Lance continued his draw, Burnett fired. Lance jerked under the impact of the heavy .45 bullet, his pistol blasting before he dropped it.

Lance's slug passed Burnett's left ear; he could not believe Lance would shoot at him. The office rocked to the thunder of the shots. Then Burnett heard a sound at his back and swung quickly, gun lifting. He froze when he saw Weedon in the doorway, in the act of dropping a gun from his suddenly lifeless hand. Weedon had a bullet hole in the centre of his forehead — Lance's bullet.

Burnett holstered his gun as Weedon fell heavily. He went to Lance's side and bent over him, fearing the worst. But Lance was conscious. Blood was seeping from his right shoulder, and Burnett knew from experience that he rarely killed with that particular shot.

'I thought you were drawing on me, Lance,' Burnett said.

'There was no time to call.' Lance spoke with difficulty. 'You should have known I wouldn't pull a gun on you.' He forced a smile.

'Don't talk now. Just take it easy.' Burnett made a rapid examination of his brother's wound. 'It's not life threatening. I'll get the doc and he'll patch you up.'

Lance closed his eyes and lapsed into unconsciousness. Burnett ran to the door, and collided with Abbie as she came to see what had happened. He sent her to fetch the doctor, and then went back to his brother, a prayer on his lips and relief in his heart.

Books by Corba Sunman
in the Linford Western Library:

RANGE WOLVES
LONE HAND
GUN TALK
TRIGGER LAW
GUNSMOKE JUSTICE
BIG TROUBLE
GUN PERIL
SHOWDOWN AT SINGING SPRINGS
TWISTED TRAIL
RAVEN'S FEUD
FACES IN THE DUST
MARSHAL LAW
ARIZONA SHOWDOWN
THE LONG TRAIL
SHOOT-OUT AT OWL CREEK
RUNNING CROOKED
HELL'S COURTYARD
KILL OR BE KILLED
READY FOR TROUBLE
BORDER FURY
PRAIRIE WOLVES
GUNSLINGER BREED
VIOLENT MEN

COLORADO CLEAN-UP
RUNNING WILD
BLOOD TRAIL
GUNS FOR GONZALEZ
SUDDEN DEATH
HELL-BENT
ROGUE SOLDIERS
GUN STORM
NEBRASKA SHOOT-OUT
RUTHLESS MEN
THE WIDELOOPERS

We do hope that you have enjoyed reading this large print book.

Did you know that all of our titles are available for purchase?

We publish a wide range of high quality large print books including:
Romances, Mysteries, Classics
General Fiction
Non Fiction and Westerns

Special interest titles available in large print are:
The Little Oxford Dictionary
Music Book, Song Book
Hymn Book, Service Book

Also available from us courtesy of Oxford University Press:
Young Readers' Dictionary
(large print edition)
Young Readers' Thesaurus
(large print edition)

For further information or a free brochure, please contact us at:
Ulverscroft Large Print Books Ltd.,
The Green, Bradgate Road, Anstey,
Leicester, LE7 7FU, England.
Tel: (00 44) **0116 236 4325**
Fax: (00 44) **0116 234 0205**

*Other titles in the
Linford Western Library:*

A FINAL SHOOT-OUT

J. D. Kincaid

When Abe Fletcher is released from prison, he's anxious to reclaim his inheritance — a beautiful and flourishing ranch. At the same time, bank robbers Red Ned Davis and Hank Jolley are fleeing from justice and holed up with Jolley's cousin, Vic Morgan. After a chance encounter between Abe and Vic, the outlaws agree to help Abe regain his inheritance — for a price. However, their plans go awry due to the unexpected intervention of a seductive saloon singer, Arizona Audrey, and the famous Kentuckian gunfighter, Jack Stone . . .

SCATTERGUN SMITH

Max Gunn

When Scattergun Smith sets out after the infamous outlaw Bradley Black, his search leads him across dangerous terrain, and every fibre of his being tells him that he is travelling headfirst into the jaws of trouble. But Black has both wronged the youngster Smith and killed innocent people, and has to pay. Scattergun is determined to catch and end the life of the ruthless outlaw before Black claims fresh victims. It will take every ounce of his renowned expertise to stop him, and prove why he is called Scattergun Smith.

CROSSROADS

Logan Winters

When a wealthy rancher mistakes K. John Landis and a cantankerous ex-saloon girl for an honourable couple and offers them the opportunity to make some much-needed money, the pair jump at the chance. In charge of the rancher's flighty daughter, and playing the role of doting husband, Landis is dragged down into the violent underworld of Crossroads. He had feared leaving town without a nickel in his jeans — now he fears he might never leave again . . .

THE MAN FROM JERUSALEM

Jack Martin

Day after day, the sun does its utmost to roast the very land upon which the dilapidated town of Jerusalem sits. Johnny Jerusalem is returning home to the town of his namesake. He'd left years ago, but no sooner is he back than the little money he has is stolen from him during a bank robbery. He sets out with a young gunslinger to find the culprits who have wronged him — but there's a posse behind them, and bandits ahead of them, and soon the bullets are flying . . .